Adventure in
WYOMING

Books in the X-Country Adventure series

Adventure in WYOMING

Bob Schaller

Baker Books

A Division of Baker Book House Co
Grand Rapids, Michigan 49516

Published by Baker Books
a division of Baker Book House Company
P.O. Box 6287, Grand Rapids, MI 49516-6287

Printed in the United States of America

ISBN 0-8010-4452-9

Library of Congress Cataloging-in-Publication Data is on file at the Library of Congress, Washington, D.C.

For current information about all releases from Baker Book House, visit our web site:

http://www.bakerbooks.com

Contents

Danger Near Devils Tower

He barely knew the man, but Adam Arlington had to trust Ron Rapp.

His life depended on it.

"Let go, now!" Rapp yelled to Adam.

After "letting go," Adam fell fifty feet down the side of Devils Tower before stopping himself with the rope he and his family were using. Adam gasped, and his lungs filled with cold air. Devils Tower, the country's first national monument, rises 1,267 feet above the Belle Fourche River Valley in northeastern Wyoming. Although the Arlingtons hadn't climbed all the way to the top, the muscles in Adam's arms and legs were burning as he adjusted his hold on the rope. A few minutes later, Adam was at the bottom of Devils Tower with his family.

"Good job, little brother," said his sister, Ashley.

"Sort of takes your breath away," remarked their mother, Anne Arlington.

Ron Rapp, a park ranger and their climbing guide at Devils Tower, came down last.

"Thanks for your time," said Alex Arlington, Adam and Ashley's father. Turning to his wife, he noted that the huge Wyoming sky was gradually growing darker as evening crept in. "Probably a good time to head back to the motor home," he said.

Mrs. Arlington nodded in agreement. It was a busy first day of vacation for the Arlingtons. At least twice each year they drove their motor home away from their family home in Washington, D.C., towing their SUV along behind so they could easily explore the states they visited. Anne Arlington, a history professor and an avid runner, and Alex Arlington, a lawyer, enjoyed getting away from their hectic schedules in D.C. and spending time together with their kids vacationing as a family.

Seventeen-year-old Ashley, a five-foot-ten basketball standout, had also started for the Thomas Jefferson High School volleyball team since her freshman year. Like the rest of her family, Ashley was athletic and liked the outdoors. She had been looking forward to climbing at Devils Tower for several weeks.

Adam was a year younger and an inch shorter than his sister, and at 135 pounds was one of the best runners on the TJHS cross-country team. His first true love, however, was computers. While Ashley enjoyed spending her extra hours with the chemistry club during the school year, Adam spent as much time as he could on the computer.

He could already fix just about any technical problem, and he was incredible at locating information on the Internet.

As Adam unhooked himself from the climbing gear he was wearing, he stared up at Devils Tower.

"I read on the Internet that, according to Native American folklore, a giant bear clawed the grooves into this mountainside while chasing several young Indian maidens," Adam said to Ashley.

His sister looked up at the grooves, which did resemble an animal's claw marks.

"That would have to have been the world's biggest bear," Ashley said with a smile.

"And the world's maddest bear, too, if he was going to rake this rock all the way around," Adam answered with a grin.

As the two looked at the beautiful monument, Ron Rapp put the climbing gear into two separate bags, slinging the larger bag over his shoulder before picking up the smaller one. He had on his own personal backpack as well and was almost overloaded by the gear.

"Let me help you with one of those," Adam offered.

"Nah, it's against the rules for visitors to carry this stuff," Ron said. "But thanks for the offer."

"You're welcome," Adam said with a shrug.

"I've got to hit the road, Mr. and Mrs. Arlington," Ron said.

"We were hoping to take you out to dinner while we're here," Mr. Arlington said. "I mentioned it to your dad."

Ron's father, Thomas Rapp, had been an attorney at Mr. Arlington's law firm until five years ago, when he became a U.S. attorney in Washington, D.C. He and Mr. Arlington had stayed in touch over the years. When the Arlingtons were getting ready for their trip to Wyoming for spring vacation, Tom Rapp gave Mr. Arlington his son's phone number and reminded him that Ron was a ranger and climbing guide at Devils Tower.

During every vacation, the Arlingtons parked their forty-foot motor home at a central location in the state they were visiting. This year they had gone right for the heart of the state: Casper, Wyoming. That way the family could take their SUV to Devils Tower in northwestern Wyoming one day; go to Cheyenne, the state capital, in the southeastern corner of the state the next day; hit the gorgeous Flaming Gorge National Recreation Area in southwest Wyoming the following day, and not have to drive the motor home, with its seven-miles-per-gallon gas mileage.

As Ron started down the path away from Devils Tower, Mr. Arlington told him again that he was welcome to join them for dinner.

"That sounds really good," Ron said. "And I am very hungry. But I'm flying my plane down from Newcastle to Cheyenne tonight, so I'll have to take a rain check on that dinner."

Mr. Arlington smiled. Ron's father also had his pilot's license and flew whenever he could squeeze in the time. Ron said his plane was smaller than his father's; it seated only two people.

"It's not a big plane, but it's always gotten me there and back," Ron, who was only twenty-three, said with a smile.

Adam walked alongside Ron in front of the rest of the Arlingtons.

"Those are some nice boots," Adam said, noticing the hiking boots Ron had quickly put on after stowing the climbing gear in the two bags.

"Thanks," Ron said. "I haven't seen a lot of them that are this shade of gray. My friends and I do a lot of extreme sports, like bungee jumping. You have to have good footwear."

"I'm not big on bungee jumping, but those boots are cool," Adam said. "I'll have to try and hit my parents up for a pair when we get home."

"What's that, Adam?" his father asked, catching just the final part of the conversation.

"Oh, nothing, Dad," Adam said, grinning as Ron stopped at a door marked "Staff Only Beyond This Point."

"Well, you certainly are quite a climber, and my family appreciates you making time for us today," Mr. Arlington said to Ron.

"Thanks," Ron said. "Working as a ranger does keep me in shape! I'll tell my father how it went when I call him tonight from Cheyenne."

"Okay," Mrs. Arlington said. "And tell him, if you would, that we'll be back in D.C. late next week, and we'll invite him over for dinner."

"Will do," Ron said with a smile. "You all have a safe trip."

"And you have a safe flight," Mr. Arlington said.

Ron headed on his way as the Arlingtons registered their completion of the climb and then piled into the SUV. "That was an absolutely beautiful drive up here," Mrs. Arlington said.

"We're going back a different way, Mom," Adam said.

"Yeah, Adam planned it all out for us again," Ashley said.

Adam had actually printed out several possible routes for the trip from D.C. to the Casper campground and for each day's sightseeing trip from Casper. For the way home that night from Devils Tower, the family would stay on the interstate.

The drive back down to Casper was breathtaking, too, with mountains to the right side of the vehicle and bluffs and prairie to the left. Just outside the towns of Edgerton and Midwest was Teapot Dome, where the family had stopped that morning on the way to Devils Tower.

It was dark by the time the family got back to the campground in Casper.

"We'll get going a little later tomorrow morning," Mrs. Arlington said as they unloaded the vehicle. "We're all tired after the trip out here and then the long day climbing today. We're not going to push it the first couple of days."

"That's good news, Mom," Ashley said, putting her arm around her mother, who stood about two inches shorter than Ashley.

"Yeah, thanks," Adam said. "I should be up by noon."

"But Adam, that offer is only good if you leave your computer off and call it a night now," his mother said with a smile.

"Just two minutes, Mom—I promise, that's all," Adam said as he headed into the motor home.

Adam's laptop was equipped with a battery pack and a wireless modem, which allowed him to log on to the Internet even when the Arlingtons were camping. The rest of the family also used Adam's laptop: Ashley to e-mail friends, and her parents to keep in touch with their offices.

"What time is it here?" Mr. Arlington asked, looking at his watch. "I've got 11:00 P.M., but that's back in the nation's capital. Is it 10:00 here?"

"It's 9:00 here," his wife said. "This is mountain time."

He only needed to look west to see a reminder—mountains ran all the way north to Montana and south into Colorado.

"Remember, Adam, just a few minutes," Mrs. Arlington reminded her son as she and Mr. Arlington headed toward their bedroom in the back of the motor home.

"Okay, Mom," Adam said as he logged on to research the state of Wyoming for a couple of minutes. Rather than read all the information he had called up, he copied some of the files and turned his computer off, just as he told his parents he would. Ashley settled in bed in the middle part of the motor home with her headphones on while she read one of the four books she had brought.

Mr. Arlington brushed his teeth and hopped onto the bed. His wife had the newspaper they had bought on the way to Teapot Dome that morning. She had done all the driving on the way to Devils Tower, so she hadn't had time to catch up on that day's news. After getting in bed, she flipped on a light and opened the front section.

As Mrs. Arlington got comfortable, Mr. Arlington picked up the TV's remote control. After going through the channels once, he settled on the news, just like he did at home in D.C. when the family wound down each evening.

Mrs. Arlington checked the markets to see how her stocks were doing. One of her computer stocks had caught up with and leapt past one of her husband's stocks, so she pointed that out to him.

"I figured you'd notice that," her husband said.

"You knew already and didn't tell me?" she asked.

"I saw it this morning," he admitted sheepishly. "I would have told you eventually."

Mrs. Arlington rolled up that section of the paper and batted him on the head playfully. But at that moment the news program flashed its breaking news bulletin banner.

"Hey, turn that up, please," Mrs. Arlington said. "I wonder if it's local or national."

Just then, the picture went to an anchorwoman.

"We're just getting information now," the newswoman said, "of the crash of a small plane that was bound for the state capital of Cheyenne."

Mrs. Arlington put down the newspaper, and Mr. Arlington sat up and moved closer to the TV.

A locator map flashed on the screen. There was a star where Cheyenne was located, and Casper was also on the map. A red arrow pointed to Newcastle, not far from Devils Tower.

"We now have Phil Ford on the phone," the newswoman said as Ford's name flashed on the screen.

"Yes, we have information that a small plane went down in the hills outside Guernsey this evening," Ford said.

"Any word on how many aboard or if there were any survivors?" the newswoman asked.

"No, Diane, we have no word on survivors at this point," Ford answered. "What we do know is that the pilot was a male in his early twenties, and that there were no other people on board when the plane went down."

Mr. and Mrs. Arlington looked at each other grimly.

"Do you think . . ." he began.

"I pray not," Mrs. Arlington said, "but how many pilots in eastern Wyoming were flying to Cheyenne this evening from Newcastle? How many this week?"

"You're right," he said, running his hand through his hair. "It's just that I don't want to assume the worst."

"Me either," his wife said, grabbing her husband's hand and squeezing it. "Let's hear what else they have to say."

"Phil, we know that Camp Guernsey, a reserve base for the U.S. Army, is located in that area," the newswoman said. "Any word from the airfield there?"

"No word from the airfield yet," Ford answered. "Camp Guernsey is east of the town, and the plane went down west of town, either in or near Guernsey State Park."

Mr. Arlington knew of Camp Guernsey and Guernsey State Park from the six years he had spent as an officer in the Army Reserves. Although he had never been there, a friend of his had, and Mr. Arlington remembered that the North Platte River ran through the park.

"There's a lot of water there," he said to his wife. "I'm not sure whether that's a good thing or a bad thing."

"We'll update you as more information becomes available," Ford was saying on the news. "I will be there with a camera crew first thing in the morning. By then, we hope to have the pilot's name, pending notification of the family."

"And to repeat," Diane said, "we do not know whether the pilot was killed—is that correct, Phil?"

"That's right," Ford said. "What we do know right now is that air control out of Cheyenne has been informed that a scheduled flight did not arrive and that the plane in question disappeared in the hills near Guernsey, where an eyewitness reported seeing what he believes to have been a plane crash."

"Thanks, Phil," the newswoman said. "And now for a look at the local weather . . ."

Mr. Arlington turned the TV off and looked at his wife.

"I can't imagine what happened," he said. "Do you think I should call Tom?"

"Yes. I'd want to know right away if something happened to Ashley or Adam," she said. "But do we know it's his son? I mean, can we be certain?"

"I hear you," he replied. "It would be awful to call Tom, worry him, and then have it not be Ron who went down. But we have to do something."

"We could call the state patrol," Mrs. Arlington suggested.

"That's what I was thinking," he said. "I'm also going to call the Cheyenne and Newcastle airports."

Mr. Arlington tried both airports but couldn't get confirmation that Ron Rapp had been the pilot of the downed plane. The person answering the phone at Newcastle said more than one plane had taken off that evening—several, in fact. Two planes had been due into Cheyenne that evening. The person who answered the phone at the Cheyenne airport, however, had been instructed not to give out any information about the crash. Mainly, he told Mr. Arlington, it was because they had no more information at that time.

Mr. Arlington told his wife what little he had learned, then called the state patrol. The woman there was very nice and told him that the Federal Aviation Administration (FAA) had just arrived and would release information the following morning. Mr. Arlington related his interest in the accident, and the woman, while understanding his concern, apologized for not being able to offer more help.

"I wish we knew more," he said after hanging up the phone.

"Me, too," Mrs. Arlington agreed. "I'm hoping for the best, but I have that sinking feeling in the bottom of my stomach."

As he pulled his pillow out from under the comforter, he turned abruptly toward her.

"What is it, Alex?" she asked.

"Anne, I have to call Tom!" he said. "I have his number here in the closet in my day planner."

"Are you sure you need to call him?" she asked. "I thought you said that there were several planes headed to Cheyenne from Newcastle. Aren't you jumping the gun a little bit?"

"No, that's not why I'm going to call him," Mr. Arlington said. "It's because he has an unlisted phone number. If the authorities are trying to call Tom, they'll have no way of getting him."

He quickly dialed the phone number he had for Thomas Rapp and let the phone ring four times.

"It's 11:15 there," he said to his wife, covering the phone with his hand and looking at his watch. On the fourth ring, an answering machine picked up. He immediately recognized Tom Rapp's voice. He left a message at the beep.

"Hi, this is Alex Arlington, and we're in Wyoming right now," he said. "I need you to call me as soon as . . ."

Just then a voice was on the other end of the line.

"Alex Arlington, do you need an attorney or something?" Mr. Rapp asked satirically.

"No, Tom, I don't," Mr. Arlington said, wishing his call was indeed such a prank. "But I sure would be happy if that were the only reason I was calling you tonight."

"What's going on? Did you see Ron?" Tom Rapp asked.

Mr. Arlington told him that he had seen Ron and that they had had a good climb with him. He proceeded to tell him about the news story and his calls to the two airports and the state patrol. Mr. Rapp sounded shaken, which was not unexpected. Mr. Arlington knew how he would feel if something might have happened to Adam or Ashley and he was the father receiving a late-night call from a concerned friend.

"I don't believe it could be Ron," Mr. Rapp said. "He really is the best pilot—a much better instinctive pilot than I am. I just flew with him about two months ago. I went out there to visit, and we had the most beautiful flight to the Jackson airport from Newcastle."

"Here, let me give you the numbers of the state patrol and the two airports," Mr. Arlington said, passing along all three phone numbers. He then explained how he didn't mean to worry him, but because his number was now unlisted, he felt he should call that night after the news.

"Thanks for thinking fast," Mr. Rapp said. "I'll call the authorities in Wyoming right away to make sure the downed pilot isn't Ron."

"Okay," Mr. Arlington said. "You have our cell phone number. If you need anything—someone to pick you up if you have to come out here, or . . . just if you need anything at all, call me back. We'll pray for you tonight."

Adam heard his father's voice in the back of the motor home and could tell he was on the phone. He tapped on the bedroom door when he heard his father start talking to his mother once again.

"Come on in," his dad said.

"Sorry I knocked so quietly," Adam said. "I didn't want to wake up Ashley. She fell asleep almost as soon as she picked up her book."

"That's fine, son," Mr. Arlington said. "What's up?"

"I was just going to ask you the same question," Adam said. "I heard you talking on the phone. I figured that it couldn't be good, seeing how it's so late, and we just got here and everything. Grandma and Grandpa are okay, right?"

"They're fine," said his dad. "It doesn't involve any of our relatives. In fact, it might not involve anyone we know."

"Well, if you say everything's all right, then that's good enough for me," Adam said, relieved. He knew it would be impolite to ask more about his dad's phone call; he and his sister had been taught even when they were little to respect other people's privacy on the phone unless it was an emergency. He said good night and began to back out of his parents' room, but his dad stopped him.

"Adam," Mr. Arlington said, "I think you should know that I was talking to Tom Rapp back home. Something has happened that may affect our vacation plans here."

Seeing the concerned look on his father's face, Adam immediately lost his feelings of relief.

"If it's not Grandma and Grandpa, then what happened back home?" he asked with a sinking feeling.

"It's not a problem at home, son, it's here," Mr. Arlington said. "An unidentified plane went down between Newcastle and Cheyenne tonight. Mom and I just heard the report on the news."

"And," Adam said worriedly, "that was Ron Rapp's flight plan after our climb today, remember?"

Mr. Arlington shook his head yes. "I know," he said. "That's why I called his father. Mr. Rapp's phone number is unlisted, and no one here could reach him if the crash involves his son. I told Mr. Rapp we'll be here for him if it is Ron and if they need us for anything at all. Let's just hope it's not Ron. Pray for their family on your way to bed, and for the downed pilot, whoever it is."

"Should I wake up Ashley and tell her?" Adam asked.

"No, let her sleep," his mother said. "There's nothing more we can do tonight anyway, and we're not even sure it is Ron who went down. Let's all get some rest now, and we'll try to find out more tomorrow morning."

"Okay," Adam said, wishing it were already tomorrow morning. Closing his parents' door behind him, Adam went out and climbed into his bed. His sister, however, was the only one who slept peacefully.

With their thoughts on Ron Rapp, he and his parents had a much harder time falling asleep.

Chapter 2

Surprise While Sightseeing

When the sun rose the next morning, Ashley was the first one up. She put out a glass of juice for each person and toasted several bagels.

"Rise and shine," Ashley yelled into the camper. "It's almost 8:00. Let's go. It's a beautiful morning, and I'm not going for a bike ride all by myself."

Mrs. Arlington smiled at her husband as he woke up. Usually during the family vacations, she served as the family's unofficial "fitness guru," deciding whether the family would bike, run, walk, or go for a swim if they were camped near water. But Ashley had already unhooked the bikes they had rented for the week and was unpacking her biking gloves as she sat down for breakfast.

Ashley was soon joined by her family at the table and chairs set up under the awning. Mrs. Arlington had parked the motor home facing east to keep away the wind and maximize the morning sunlight. As Mr. Arlington reached for his juice, the phone rang inside.

He and his wife just looked at each other for a second.

"I can get it—I'm already up," Ashley said.

"Thank you, Ashley, but I think I had better get this one," Mr. Arlington said as he rushed toward the cell phone in the front of the camper.

The family couldn't hear what Mr. Arlington was saying on the phone. Mrs. Arlington started to fill Ashley in on what they had seen on the news the night before and told her that her dad had called Tom Rapp, Ron's father.

Mr. Arlington came out of the motor home with a bleak look on his face. Although everyone knew what he was going to say, the words still stung.

"That was Tom," he said. "He just received the call. It was Ron's plane that went down."

Mr. Arlington sat back down at the table. He toyed with a bagel for a minute, then put it down. After taking a swallow of orange juice, he tightened his grip on the glass and addressed his family.

"No confirmation on what has happened to Ron," he said. "Tom is trying to get out here tonight, but he's having a hard time booking a flight because of the pilots' strike."

"But he has his own little plane," Mrs. Arlington said. "He could just . . ."

"That crossed my mind, too, but he's in no shape to fly. He admitted on the phone that he would only be a danger to himself and others right now if he went up in the air alone," Mr. Arlington said. "He's too preoccupied."

"That's understandable," Ashley said.

"Well, all the authorities could tell him at this point was that it was Ron's plane; they made the identification from the letters and numbers on the tail when they found it," he continued.

"What about Ron?" Adam asked.

"That's a good question," his dad said. "There's no word on whether there was a survivor."

"Does that mean he's dead?" Adam asked.

"Not necessarily," Mr. Arlington quickly replied. "It could mean that while the authorities have found the wreckage, they just haven't found Ron yet. It's just too hard to speculate. The only information we have right now is that they know Ron's plane went down near Guernsey Reservoir in the hills and that they have found Ron's wallet inside the plane. They didn't say how bad the wreck was or if the plane was in pieces. But that wouldn't be unusual for this kind of accident, especially in a remote area in a state so sparsely populated. The authorities are doing the best they can. It's just too early to have the answers to a lot of questions that all of us, especially Ron's dad, are asking."

"What can we do?" Ashley asked. "We could help if we went up there. I know there's a lot of water in that area, but Adam and I are good swimmers. And even though there are hills, we're all good hikers."

"Your intentions are certainly good, and I'm proud of you for that," Mrs. Arlington said. "But I'm sure they have trained search teams in the area. The last thing we should do is get in their way."

"Yes, and Tom won't know anything else until this afternoon when the FAA team examines the site," Mr. Arlington added. "I'd say the best thing we could do is say a prayer for Ron and Tom and try to just go about our day as planned."

"Maybe a little exercise will help clear our minds and lend some perspective to the whole situation," Mrs. Arlington said. "Let's go ahead and get the morning workout in before we head to Cheyenne."

"Good idea," Mr. Arlington said. "We'll finish eating, go for a ride, get cleaned up, and then head out for the day. We can check messages whenever we stop."

The wind was not as strong as the day before, which made for a nice bike ride. After that the family got cleaned up back at the motor home before hitting the road for Cheyenne. Arriving in the state capital, the Arlingtons took a walking tour of the historic downtown area. Although they enjoyed seeing the golden-domed capitol building, Cheyenne wasn't as big as the Arlingtons expected it to be.

"For a state capital, it still seems like a smaller town in a lot of ways," Adam observed.

"I noticed that, too," his mother said. "And I'll bet the people here like it that way."

"You know, the University of Wyoming is less than fifty miles from here. We could go and check it out," Ashley said. "They have good academic programs, and their sports teams play in the Western Athletic Conference."

"That's not a bad idea," Mr. Arlington said. "We'll go if we have time." He and Mrs. Arlington enjoyed college visits almost as much as their kids did.

Before leaving Cheyenne, Mr. Arlington used the cell phone to check messages. Sure enough, there was one from Thomas Rapp. Mr. Arlington listened quietly, then relayed its contents.

"Tom hasn't been able to get out of D.C. yet," he said. "Every time he gets close to leaving, the FAA or Wyoming state authorities call wanting to know more information. Still no word on Ron. Tom wants to fly out of D.C. tonight. He'll have to connect out of Denver and then into Cheyenne."

"I can only imagine what he's going through," Ashley said. "I wish we could do more!"

"We all do," Mrs. Arlington said, turning sideways in the front passenger seat so she could look at both her children and her husband. "But since we can't for now, how about we go east on I-80 instead of west? Adam, you said you saw on the Internet that the area in extreme southeastern Wyoming is dotted with the U.S. Air Force's missile silos. Shall we take a look at them?"

"Yeah, Mom, I did mention that," Adam said. "And that would be great. After that, we could head back toward Casper on U.S. 26."

Mr. Arlington looked at the map. "Perfect," he said. "We can visit Fort Laramie on the way."

"Fort Laramie!" Ashley said. "I can't wait to visit there. That's the one place, along with Yellowstone and the Tetons, that I really want to see."

Though chemistry was her favorite subject, Ashley had inherited a love of history from her mother. Mrs. Arlington had a talent for making history "come alive," surprising her college history students back home by actually getting them interested in the history lectures she presented. She had entertained Ashley and Adam, too—more often than not while growing up, their bedtime story at night was an exciting or amusing incident taken from Professor Arlington's history class lectures given earlier that day. They couldn't wait to actually see some of the places that their mother had already taken them to in their imaginations when they were small.

"Fort Laramie was one of the big outposts back in the 1800s," Ashley informed the others. "It's where two treaties were negotiated with the Indians and where the Indians would get supplies from the U.S. soldiers. The barracks and some other buildings there are still standing. And in 1996 an X ray taken down by the North Platte River found an old dump that contained buttons from soldiers' coats and that kind of thing."

"And from there," Mr. Arlington said, "we're only about twenty-five miles from Guernsey. We'll stop there and see if we can find some sort of status report on Ron's crash."

The ride on I-80 was beautiful. At several points, only the prairie could be seen in any direction. The occasional houses that dotted the landscape were isolated. When the family arrived in Pine Bluffs, they stopped to see the Pine Bluffs historic cliff dwellings and digging areas. That took about an hour, putting the time at noon. They decided not to eat until Fort Laramie because they wanted to arrive in Guernsey before it got dark.

After leaving Pine Bluffs and reaching an area of beautiful hills and trees near Albin, the family saw a missile silo close to the road. Mr. Arlington stopped, and they all got out.

From the gate near the road, they could see what looked like three manhole covers. The huge one was for the missile. The two smaller ones were for entering and exiting the underground base. In addition to the gate near the road, the cemented silo area was fenced in with barbed wire across the top. A white missile-like statue stood inside the fenced area.

"If they put these missiles out here to hide them from Soviet spies, they didn't do a very good job," Adam said with a smile.

The sign said to keep out, and the Arlingtons did just that. That proved to be a good decision; as they got back in the SUV, two dark blue trucks with the words "U.S. Air Force" painted in yellow on the side drove up. The three enlisted men and two women waved to the Arlingtons as they went through the open gate, closing it after the second vehicle went through. The airmen opened the hatch when they got to the concrete area, and two other young airmen emerged.

"Wow, that must be something to live down there for a week or so at a time," Adam said.

Mrs. Arlington was driving now, and she pulled the SUV back out on the highway. As they headed past the tiny town of Hawk Springs, the family marveled at the bluffs to the west.

"All that prairie and those bluffs—it doesn't look like anyone lives out here," Adam said.

"Oh, I'd say some folks do, judging by the No Tres-passing signs we can see," his mom replied.

"I still think it would be great to live out here. No one would bother you," Adam said.

"Yeah, I know what you mean," said his dad, "and I think that's the idea."

Unable to control their hunger anymore, the Arlingtons stopped in Lingle to eat and pick up a tourist guide book. While there, they learned of a memorial on a little-known road just outside of town.

They took the road and, after a couple of miles, found the small historical marker. The marker served as a memorial to Second Lieutenant John L. Grattan and his men. On the marker was a plaque that read:

In memory of Brevet 2nd Lieutenant John L. Grattan of the Sixth U.S. Infantry and the men under his command, who died near this spot on August 19, 1854. Commanding a detachment of 29 soldiers and an interpreter, Lieutenant Grattan was sent to arrest a Miniconjou Indian for supposedly stealing an emigrant's cow.

It is unknown exactly what transpired in the Brule Indian camp 8 miles east of Fort Laramie that day, but no settlement satisfactory to both sides would be reached, and fighting broke out. The battle claimed the lives of Grattan and his detachment, as well as of Chief Conquering Bear.

Historians refer to this incident as the first major battle of the Northern Plains Indian Wars. Let this memorial stand as a reminder to all peoples to "bear with one another, forgiving each other," so as to live long and peacefully together upon this land.

The sign didn't mention that the Indians admitted killing the cow and offered dozens of horses as compensation when the U.S. Army came after them. But the army insisted that the cow killer be arrested. When the Indians wouldn't agree, the army wanted to fight. In the battle that ensued the Sioux Indians, who may have numbered up to 4,000 in the camp, wiped out everyone under the command of Grattan, including Grattan himself, who had long boasted that he needed only a handful of soldiers to rid the plains of Indians forever. Grattan, as it turned out, was wrong.

The field where the battle had taken place was now home to row upon row of corn. The Arlingtons pondered the memorial quietly, then resumed their journey to Fort Laramie.

As they exited left off the small highway, they saw an old wooden bridge that lay only a few yards from the bridge that they were about to cross. They pulled over, stopping where metal bars kept vehicles from crossing the wooden structure. A sign said the bridge was over a hundred years old. The Arlingtons walked across it and stopped in the middle, watching the water of the North Platte River pass underneath.

"I wonder what it would have been like to be one of the soldiers assigned to Fort Laramie back then," Adam said. "At least they could come to the river to bathe and fish each day."

"And I wonder what it would have been like to be a Native American coming to collect water, bathe, or fish," said Ashley. "Imagine seeing the soldiers and so many settlers there too, doing the same, where before there had only been your people or a few neighboring tribes to contend with."

"It was a difficult time for everyone," Mrs. Arlington said, "and the wounds aren't all healed even now."

Mr. Arlington and Mrs. Arlington continued on holding hands and walking all the way across the bridge and back before stopping in the middle to wait for Ashley and Adam.

The Arlingtons visited Fort Laramie, which was everything Ashley expected and more. Several bunkhouses had been refurbished, but still had original beds inside. The jailhouse looked as scary as it must have been in the old days. Various supply buildings were also intact, as were a few of the officers' residences. These were spacious, especially when compared to the enlisted men's living quarters.

The Arlingtons headed back to the highway, making the final trek to Guernsey. The hills west of Guernsey were forested. Just south of the highway was the North Platte River, lined with the green of trees and bushes as it wound its way toward Nebraska to the east.

"You could hop in a raft, and they wouldn't ever find you," Adam said with a laugh. "People would wonder what happened to you."

Everyone in the SUV laughed. They were passing Camp Guernsey on their left, entering town from the east, when their laughs disappeared—a flatbed truck was coming down the hill west of town near the entrance to Guernsey State Park.

What appeared to have been an airplane was now scrap metal, stacked up like a deck of cards on the back of the truck.

"Oh no! Alex, you don't think that could be—" Mrs. Arlington hesitated to say what they were all thinking. "*Could* it be Ron's plane?" she finally managed in a shaky voice.

It was amazing, Mr. Arlington thought, that these scraps of metal used to be anyone's airplane. And it would be a miracle if anyone had survived such a horrible crash.

"Excuse me!" he yelled, rolling down his window and waving his arm for the truck driver to stop. The truck did stop, and the driver leaned out the window of the truck's cab.

"Are you lost?" he asked Mr. Arlington.

"No, I just saw the wreckage you have there on the back. Is that from the crash we heard about last night, and do you know if the pilot, Ron Rapp, survived?" Mr. Arlington asked.

"All I know about this crash is what I heard on the radio," the driver said. "I thought at first it might have been a military plane crash. This is the week hundreds of army reservists come to Camp Guernsey, and the airfield out there has more planes and helicopters on it than you could shake a stick at. But it's a civilian plane. I don't know if that pilot you mentioned survived, but it was his plane all right. I have to drop this thing off at a hangar at the Cheyenne airport as soon as I can. There are cars coming, Sir, so I've gotta get going."

"Okay, thanks," Mr. Arlington said, rolling up his window. He turned right toward the entrance to Guernsey State Park—and toward the crash site.

Dent in the Mountain

Mr. Arlington pulled into the park entrance and stopped as a park ranger came out of the entrance booth.

"Hi," she said. "Are you staying for the night?"

"No, we're not," he said. "We're just going to visit for an hour or two."

"All right," she said. "Then all you need is a day pass. But we'd like to ask you to stay out of this area of the hills."

The ranger pointed to a map, circled part of it near the water, and handed the map to Mr. Arlington.

"We had a small plane crash up here last night," the ranger said.

"Was anyone injured?" Mr. Arlington asked.

"I've been asked that question at least fifty times today, and I just don't know the answer," the ranger said. "All I know is that visitors need to stay away from the circled area."

"Okay," he said. "Thank you."

"Thank you," the ranger said. "And have a nice visit."

The Arlingtons headed down a hill into the park. Mr. Arlington pulled to the side of the road and stopped at the Guernsey Dam, listening to the roar of the water as it was released through the dam.

"We'll go down there on our way out of the park and get a closer look," Mrs. Arlington said to Ashley and Adam.

Mr. Arlington guided the SUV around a continuous series of curves in the road until they saw a sheriff's vehicle turn onto a dirt road. Since the road was not marked off-limits, he decided to follow the car. Up the road at a clearing was a gathering of several emergency and government vehicles. He pulled off the road and parked. The family got out of the SUV and walked toward the hill, where they could now see that a large area had been roped off by the emergency workers.

They walked to the base of the hill through the deep grass and stopped at the ropes. A fresh clearing on the hillside obviously marked the crash site. The plane had cleared out several trees, but remarkably didn't appear to have started a fire or burned anything in the area. One of the seats from the plane was still in the new clearing. The most startling feature about the crash site was the exact spot where the plane had apparently hit. It had left a dent in the mountain like a wrecking ball had been slammed into the spot.

"If Ron was in that plane when it hit," Mrs. Arlington said, looking toward the rest of the family, "there would be nothing left of him. I can't imagine that he could've survived it."

"It looks like the plane came in on a line drive and just drilled the hill," Mr. Arlington said. "To leave that kind of mark, it definitely wasn't brought down under any kind of control."

Surrounding the area were police, state patrol officers, and others who appeared to be government workers wearing windbreakers. A woman motioned to them to stay back.

"Please, stop exactly where you are!" she said.

The whole family stayed put as the woman hurried over.

"Folks, we have an investigation going on here," said the woman. "Please, we can't run the risk of you accidentally destroying any evidence by walking into this area."

"I'm Alex Arlington," Mr. Arlington said, extending his hand to the woman. "We didn't mean to intrude on the search. This is my wife, Anne, and these are our two kids, Ashley and Adam. We know the young man who was piloting the downed plane."

The woman nodded and introduced herself as Julie Mitchum, an FAA investigator.

"You know his name?" she asked.

"Yes, we believe the pilot was Ron Rapp," Mr. Arlington answered.

Mitchum nodded. "Right. I just wanted to make sure you really did know the pilot."

"I'm an attorney, and I used to work with Ron's father, Thomas," Mr. Arlington said. "We're close friends of theirs, out here on vacation."

"I've talked to Thomas Rapp several times today," Mitchum said, taking off her blue FAA cap to reveal long, blond hair. She rearranged her hair and put the cap on over it again. "Mr. Rapp is probably going to head out here tomorrow."

"Yes, that's the message he left us," Mr. Arlington said. "Can you give us any news about Ron?"

"Mr. and Mrs. Arlington, we're at a loss trying to figure out what happened here," Mitchum said, locking her fingers together and putting her hands behind her neck. "You see, we've been through all the wreckage and even loaded it on a truck so we can analyze it down at a hangar in Cheyenne. We have the wings and rudder, everything from the plane. But we have seen no sign of the pilot."

"No pilot?" Mrs. Arlington repeated. "Where could Ron be?"

"We're asking ourselves the same question, and we don't have an answer," Mitchum said. "Judging by the wreckage, this plane came down hard and fast. It's hard to imagine that someone survived the crash, much less got up and walked away."

"Amazing," Mr. Arlington said. "So, do you believe Ron Rapp is still alive?"

"We have no idea," Mitchum said. "We don't have any really good theories to operate on here; everything we've come up with is just so improbable. There's no obvious answer, yet no sign of the pilot's body. But, we do understand that the pilot was in very good shape."

"I'll say he was," Adam said. "He was our climbing guide at Devils Tower yesterday. He's got muscles in his arms and legs that you wouldn't believe."

"You saw him yesterday?" Mitchum asked.

"We sure did, for several hours," Ashley spoke up.

"Did he say anything about his plans last evening?" Mitchum asked, pulling a notebook out of her back pocket and grabbing a pen.

"Yes," Mrs. Arlington recalled. "He said he was flying from Newcastle to Cheyenne last night. In fact, we had asked Ron's father before we came out here if he'd extend a dinner invitation to Ron for us. Ron said yesterday that he'd have to take a rain check on dinner because he had already made plans to fly to Cheyenne; so we put dinner with him off until another time."

"I see," Mitchum said. "Did he seem preoccupied?"

"Just the opposite," Mr. Arlington said. "He took us on a tough climb, really the kind that stops your heart for a minute. And he was excited about flying last night."

"Do you remember what he was wearing?" Mitchum asked.

"I do," Adam said. "He had on these really cool gray hiking boots when he changed out of his climbing shoes. He was still wearing tan shorts, and he had taken off the shirt he wore to climb and put on a black T-shirt as we walked away from Devils Tower."

"That's pretty good, Adam," his mother said, putting her hand on her son's shoulder. "That's a lot better description than I could have done."

"I just remember the boots because I'd like to get a pair," Adam said.

"Thanks, Adam," Mitchum said. "This may help us identify him if we find him. We've checked his flight records in the computer," she continued. "He appears to have been a pretty solid pilot. There were no complaints or reports of any recklessness or misconduct in the air."

"His father told me the same thing last night," Mr. Arlington said.

"Last night?" Mitchum asked.

"Yes, my wife and I saw the story about the crash on the news, and our worst fear when we saw the locator map was that it involved Ron," he said. "We called Tom to let him know about the report and that there was a chance it could involve Ron. Tom has an unlisted number, so we suspected that the authorities here might have trouble getting in touch with him."

"That was good thinking," Mitchum said. "Mr. Rapp called the state patrol in Wyoming just when I was getting ready to have the authorities in D.C. find him."

"Well, his father said Ron is an excellent pilot," Mr. Arlington related. "Tom himself is an outstanding flier, and he said that Ron was even better. I've flown with Tom, and he seems pretty top-notch."

"That's why none of this is making sense," Mitchum said. "From everything we've heard this guy is really a neat, well-adjusted person with a lot of interests. We've heard no reports of depression or anything else that would indicate a suicide."

"Oh, if you met Ron, I imagine you would rule that out," Mrs. Arlington said.

"Do you have any reason to think that drugs or alcohol may have been an issue?" Mitchum asked.

"We don't know him well anymore since he moved to Wyoming from D.C., but I don't think so," Ashley said. "Judging by the condition he's in, I don't think he would abuse his body that way."

"I didn't mean any disrespect," Mitchum said. "It's standard procedure to check into that issue for anyone involved in a crash."

"We understand," Mr. Arlington said. "You must be racking your brains for any sort of answer."

"We've all been doing that," Mitchum said. "All day long. But now we have more questions than we did earlier and still not an answer in sight. Did Rapp have anything with him when you saw him leaving Devils Tower— a suitcase, anything like that?"

"I just saw his blue backpack," Adam said. "He was carrying two other bags when we headed for the souvenir shop, but those had his climbing gear and the stuff we used to climb yesterday."

"Let me give you our cell phone number," Mr. Arlington said. "Feel free to call us if we can help."

"That would be great," Mitchum said. "Could you come with me over to where the command post is set up? I'd like to introduce you to some of the people working for me."

They went over, and Mr. Arlington repeated part of their story. A couple of the searchers asked additional questions and then brought Mitchum up-to-date on their search efforts as the Arlingtons listened in. The searchers told Mitchum that no one had seen any footprints walking away from the crash site—in any direction. A sheriff's deputy standing nearby also said that two tracking dogs were on the way to see if they could pick up a scent.

"Ms. Mitchum," Mr. Arlington broke in, "do you think Ron could have possibly parachuted to safety before the impact?"

"Absolutely," Mitchum replied, "except that it has been twenty-four hours. He should have turned up by now if he survived the crash, or at least been found if he's injured and immobile. We've covered a lot of ground already, with no signs of him yet."

"I wondered about that, too, and it concerns me," Mrs. Arlington said. "If he was alive and well he would want to let his father know he's safe and check on his plane, which he is very attached to—or was," she finished quietly.

"We can't rule out that he parachuted to safety, of course, but given the circumstances since the crash, it doesn't seem likely at this point. Yet he's certainly not here at the site of impact," Mitchum said. "We'll just keep looking for puzzle pieces till we have them all."

Mitchum thanked the Arlingtons, and the family shook hands with the dozen or so searchers, law enforcement officers, FAA agents, and other park employees they had just met.

After walking back to the SUV, the Arlingtons paused as they waited for Mr. Arlington to unlock the doors.

"Anyone got any theories?" he asked.

"I do—that people think better where it's warm," his wife said with a shiver. The lighthearted moment made them all laugh. And she was right—it was getting chilly as the wind blew off the crystal blue water of the Guernsey Reservoir.

Mr. Arlington opened the doors, and they all fastened their seat belts as he started the vehicle and turned it around on the road.

"I wish we had brought the tent and the other camping gear with us," Ashley said. "Then we could stay down here tonight."

"I'm not sure that would have been the best idea," her mother said. "The authorities are looking for clues, and any clue that is damaged by an untrained searcher could be rendered useless."

"I know, Mom," Ashley said. "But this is the son of one of Dad's friends—someone who has been coming to our house for dinner since I was really little. I just wish there was more we could do."

"I know," her mom said quietly. "I do, too."

"I'm really confused by this whole thing," Adam said. "He's not in the plane, not around the plane, no one spotted a parachute, and no one has seen or heard from him. There aren't even any footprints. Even for the best detective, that's not much to go on."

"It seems like there has to be something else involved," Ashley said.

"That's my thought, too," their father said. "I'm not saying it's foul play, but I can't rule it out, either. Like the investigators at Guernsey said, they can't rule anything in or out until they have more information."

"It just seems so implausible to me that Ron could be involved in any trouble," Mrs. Arlington said.

"I can't believe that, either," Adam added.

With nothing more to contribute to the search, the Arlingtons decided to head back to their campground. The up-and-down ride through the hills outside of Casper kept Adam and Ashley awake until they arrived at the motor home a little after 10:00 P.M.

"We have a couple of messages," Mrs. Arlington said as she checked the voice mail. She turned up the volume on the cell phone, and everyone stopped what they were doing to listen.

"Alex and Anne, this is Tom Rapp," said the voice on the machine, speaking haltingly and taking a deep breath with each pause. "I'm still trying to get out there; this airline strike has slowed me down, and I'm not in the emotional state where I can fly my own plane. But I should be in Wyoming tomorrow. I'll check back soon. Thanks."

The Arlingtons looked at each other as the second message started.

"Hello, it's me again," said the familiar voice of Tom Rapp. "It's about midnight here, and I have a message from the woman with whom you spoke today, a Julie Mitchum. She says they have a traveler who thinks he saw Ron this evening. A train yard employee in the area also confirmed the sighting of a young man who fits Ron's description. I don't know what to make of it all. Call me when you get in. Thanks."

Since it was only 10:15 P.M. mountain time, Mr. Rapp's message was about fifteen minutes old.

"I'm going to call him right away," Mr. Arlington said, heading to the back of the motor home to get the number from his planner. He called, and Mr. Rapp answered the phone before the first ring was even completed.

"Hi, Tom, it's Alex," he said.

"Alex, you got my messages, right?" Mr. Rapp asked.

"We did," he said.

"I don't know what to think," Mr. Rapp said. "I'm almost equal parts concerned, confused, relieved, and scared. Someone at Camp Guernsey, a reservist who had just arrived for his two weeks of summer duty, was pulling into town. Apparently, there's a bridge just west of town near a big railroad yard."

"Yes, we went over it; I'm familiar with it," Mr. Arlington said.

"Well, this reservist sees a guy about six-foot-one, 175 pounds, with short red hair and wearing a black T-shirt and shorts—he wasn't sure of the color of the shorts—hopping over the tracks. The reservist sees the train activity and slows down his car to honk at this guy. Supposedly, he yelled to the guy to watch out, that he had seen two or three trains headed that way during the past fifteen minutes or so as he headed toward Guernsey. Basically, he was trying to warn this guy on the tracks. Then one of the train yard workers caught sight of the guy, too, and he described him in the same way."

"This guy on the tracks sounds like Ron," Mr. Arlington said.

"Well, the description does sound similar, but Ron's at least an inch and a half shorter than that."

"Tom, Adam remembered that Ron had on a black T-shirt and tan shorts; he told that to the investigators at the crash site."

"Thank God! It means Ron probably is still alive! I'm going to call Julie Mitchum right now. Hopefully she can give me some more details."

"Good idea," Mr. Arlington said. "Keep us posted if you can."

"I will. I can't tell you how relieved I am, knowing Ron probably survived. But now there are just more questions. Where could Ron be, and is he all right?"

"That's what we were talking about on the way back from Guernsey," Mr. Arlington said.

"Well, I'll call you as soon as I get a flight out there. Good night, and thanks, Alex."

After hanging up, Mr. Arlington briefed his family on the conversation.

"It sure sounds like Ron is alive," Ashley said.

"You're right—that's the important thing," Adam said. "But if he is alive, what's going on? Where is he? How did he escape the crash? Why hasn't he called anyone? Does he have amnesia or something? This whole thing is really weird."

"I can't believe they saw him at the train yard outside of Guernsey," Ashley said. "I wonder what time the sighting was; we were just there today."

"That railroad had quite a presence in a small town like Guernsey," Mr. Arlington said. "I always liked trains when I was growing up. I could sit on a hill looking down on a rail yard like that all day, just watching the trains coming in and out and the engines moving rail cars around the yard."

"I wonder if Ron likes trains, too," Adam said. "It must be at least two or three miles from the crash site to the rail yard."

"If it really *was* Ron at the rail yard," Ashley said.

Adam turned on his laptop and called up a map of Wyoming on his computer screen. As his mom looked at the screen over his shoulder, Ashley and her father pulled out an atlas.

"There's not much doubt that Ron came in from the north," Ashley said. "Does everyone agree with me on that?"

"Definitely," Adam said. "He came down from Newcastle, which is due north of Guernsey."

"Okay," Ashley said. "But that hill they found the airplane on . . . wasn't that hill facing south, meaning Ron's plane was actually traveling north, not south, when it slammed into the side of the hill?"

"That's a good observation," their father said. "You're absolutely right."

"From the south?" Adam asked. "What in the world would he be doing flying north at that point in his trip?"

Mrs. Arlington looked at the map and did some figuring in her mind.

"Ron would have been about three-fourths of the way to Cheyenne at that point," she said. "Why would he turn around?"

"We have one more clue—that he was heading north—but we also have about ten more mysteries," Adam said, shaking his head.

"I feel so sorry for Mr. Rapp, not knowing what's going on with his son—or even if Ron is, for sure, alive," Ashley said.

"Let's call it a night," their father said. "A good night's sleep might clear our heads a little. We've had a lot of information to digest. But, before we do that, let's talk about tomorrow."

"We aren't going to help with the search or anything like that?" Ashley asked.

"I don't think so," Mrs. Arlington said. "Unless we are asked, it wouldn't be appropriate. We're really limited as to what we can offer in this situation. Besides, we're heading the opposite way tomorrow, remember? We're going on an overnight trip to Flaming Gorge, then to the Wind River Indian Reservation near Riverton the following morning, and then to the hot springs in Thermopolis before we come back here."

"That'll be fun," Ashley said.

"Yes, it should be," Mr. Arlington said. "I'll go ahead and put the sleeping bags, tent, propane lamps, backpacks, and everything else we'll need in the back of the SUV tonight so we can get out of here at a reasonable hour in the morning."

"Dad, if you want to stay here and wait for Mr. Rapp to arrive from home, we'll understand," Adam said. "We could find things to do around this area, I'm sure."

"That's right," Ashley agreed. "You don't have to take us sightseeing and entertain us. We can stay here to help Mr. Rapp when he arrives."

"I thought about that after he called," Mr. Arlington said. "But like your mother said, there's really nothing more we can do at this point. We'll have our cell phone along for the ride, and as soon as Mr. Rapp calls me with his flight information, we can head back to meet him if necessary. We'll do all we can to help him as the investigation progresses, but in the meantime we might as well enjoy our vacation."

His family shook their heads in agreement, even though everyone was frustrated that they couldn't do more at the moment to help Ron and his father.

Mr. Arlington quickly loaded the SUV. Mrs. Arlington read, sitting outside under the awning of the camper, while Ashley and Adam readied themselves for bed. Adam reconfirmed the travel plans on his computer and checked for road construction to make sure the trip would be as smooth as possible, something his parents—and Ashley, for that matter—really appreciated him doing. He had saved them a lot of downtime on the roads that way on their many vacations in the motor home.

As Adam logged off and crawled into bed, he couldn't help wondering about the trip their friend Ron seemed to be taking. Adam said a quiet prayer for his safety before falling asleep.

Railway Runaway

The following day's mountainous trek began at about 8:00 A.M., after a five-mile run just after sunrise and a breakfast of fresh fruit, toast, juice, and milk. The Arlingtons went through Muddy Gap before heading west on Interstate 80 toward Flaming Gorge. They stopped in Rock Springs and read the town's newspaper, the *Rock Springs Daily Rocket-Miner,* as they ate lunch. Exiting in Green River, the Arlingtons stopped at a local grocery store to get supplies, including food and ice for the cooler, before arriving in the Flaming Gorge National Recreation Area early in the afternoon.

The family checked in and then parked the SUV. Often on other trips, they had hiked to the middle of what seemed to be nowhere to pitch the tent. This time they decided they'd keep it simple. They set the tent up not ten yards from the SUV, meaning this time there would be no long hike to a remote campsite carrying heavy backpacks. With the sleeping bags and air mattresses set up in the tent, the Arlingtons decided to explore the area on foot.

After hiking for nearly four hours and drinking water at every stop, the Arlingtons made their way back to camp. As darkness started to crawl in slowly, Mrs. Arlington got a fire going, and Mr. Arlington and Ashley cooked a dinner of beans and hot dogs. Adam took care of unloading the potato chips and soda, and they enjoyed their outdoor meal.

After cleaning up and putting out the cooking fire, the family walked to the shore of Flaming Gorge Reservoir. They walked along the shore for nearly a mile before turning back toward the campground to retire for the evening.

With two lamps on, they settled down for some reading. Sometimes, one parent would read to the whole family. However, Adam had been the most prepared for this trip, and he read out loud about Jesse James's infamous time in Wyoming, including his stint in jail.

After about forty-five minutes, the propane lamps were turned off. On occasion, the lamps had been left on just for the heat they gave off. However, although it was windy in Wyoming earlier that day, it wasn't very cold at bedtime. It would be a quiet night, except for the sound of the waves gently greeting the shore of the reservoir in a rhythmic pattern.

Ashley and Adam woke just after sunrise the following morning. While the custom on vacation was almost always for a morning family exercise session, Ashley and Adam decided to head out on their own and let their parents sleep in. After a five-mile run along the shore, they were shocked to find their parents still asleep well past 7:00 A.M.

"Let's get breakfast going and surprise them," Ashley said. "It would be nice if we got things going today and let them relax like they always do for us."

"I don't think so," Adam said. "With Mom and Dad sleeping in, this is my chance to spend some time on my computer early in the day for once. Don't you ever get tired of racing around to exercise, eating a healthy breakfast, and getting on schedule first thing in the morning, Ash? We get enough of that during school! Let's break out the sugared cereal."

"I'm surprised at you, Adam. It's a wonder you're so good at cross-country with that attitude," Ashley retorted. "You'll probably be a couch potato when you're old and out of school if that's all the self-discipline you have when you don't *have* to do things!"

"You've got me there, and I do plan on being a couch potato some of my life, or at least an Internet addict," Adam laughed, punching his annoyed sister playfully in the arm.

"Ouch! Adam, stop it. Mom and Dad have done a lot for us taking us on these vacations. Let's do something nice for them instead of hitting each other."

"Hitting each other?" he said. "You didn't hit me yet."

"I will if you don't help me get this surprise breakfast going," Ashley threatened.

"Okay, okay, I'll have to be lazy some other time, I guess. I'll do bacon and eggs if you do toast and set up everything," Adam proposed.

"That's a deal," Ashley said with a smile. She got the cooking fire going as Adam unloaded the needed ingredients from the SUV. He cooked eight eggs and nearly a whole pack of bacon while Ashley took care of everything else. Just then they heard a whisper in the tent. It was their mother waking up their father.

"I don't know why," they could hear their dad saying, "but it sure does smell good out there."

Ashley and Adam laughed. They heard the rustling in the tent as their parents put on their shoes.

"Well, what are you two up to?" their mom asked with a smile, as their dad zipped up the tent to keep bugs out.

"We just thought it was our turn to handle everything," Ashley said.

"You two already exercised this morning?" Mr. Arlington asked.

"According to the time and the pace I estimated, I'd say we did just over five miles," Ashley said.

"Incredible," their mom said. "Our kids are now the U.S. Army—they do more before 9:00 A.M. than we'll do all day!"

They all shared a laugh and then sat down for a good breakfast.

"Well, Adam, it looks like you'll be handling the cooking duties when we get home," Mrs. Arlington said as she and her husband finished clearing their plates.

"Fine with me," Adam answered. "But Ashley did help— a little."

This time Ashley punched Adam in the arm, but it wasn't playfully.

"Watch it, you two!" their father warned. "Your mother and I will take care of the cleaning," he then added.

"How about we do the cleaning, and you and Mom can just go for a walk, since we've already done our running for the morning?" Ashley suggested.

"Works for me," Mrs. Arlington said. "But work *together*, okay? As full as I am, I couldn't do much more than a walk right now."

As their parents set off hand in hand, Ashley and Adam cleaned up the campsite. Their parents were still not back when the cleaning was done, so they decided to break camp and load the SUV.

"Man, we could really get used to this," their father said in surprise when he and Mrs. Arlington returned from their walk. He looked at his watch and added, "We're way ahead of schedule, so maybe we can make a few unscheduled stops before we get all set up in Riverton tonight."

"We're staying at a campground in a town tonight?" Ashley asked.

"No," Mrs. Arlington answered. "We were going to surprise you two. But since you already surprised us so pleasantly, we'll tell you now. We're not going to camp tonight. We'll do that tomorrow in Thermopolis. Tonight, we're going to stay at a bed-and-breakfast I found on the Internet when we were planning this trip."

"Awesome," Ashley said. "That'll be a nice change of pace from camping, even though I love to camp."

They dumped a bunch of trash when they stopped in the town of Green River. Adam and his mother, who was driving, went over the best route for their day. They would exit at Rock Springs and take U.S. 191 north past Eden to State Highway 28. They would stay on that all the way to Sinks Canyon State Park in the Shoshone National Forest, which they wanted to visit. After lunch in Lander, they would travel for less than half an hour before reaching Riverton, the only incorporated city within the borders of the Wind River Indian Reservation.

Mrs. Arlington exited in Rock Springs and stopped at a convenience store. While Adam checked the oil and coolant under the hood, Ashley filled the gas tank. Mrs. Arlington went inside to pick up beverages and pay for the gas. Mr. Arlington stepped outside and used the cell phone to check voice mail messages.

After they had done their share of the work, Adam and Ashley got back in the SUV. Their mom returned with bottled water for everyone, but their dad was still on the phone. He was running his hand through his hair, which his family recognized as an indication that he was deep in thought.

As he walked toward the SUV, he looked very preoccupied. He climbed into the front passenger seat, and Mrs. Arlington handed him a bottle of water.

"Thanks," he said. "You guys aren't going to believe this one."

"We had messages?" his wife asked.

"Two," he said. "The first was from Tom at about 4:30 this morning. He didn't have any new word on Ron, but he was going to leave Dulles International Airport at about 7:00 A.M. on a flight to Cheyenne."

"We're a few hours from Cheyenne," Mrs. Arlington said. "But it's right on I-80. If we start heading there now, we'll be in Cheyenne this afternoon."

"He won't be in Cheyenne," he said.

"But, Dad," Adam said, "you said he had a flight and everything, right?"

"The second message was from an attorney who worked with both Mr. Rapp and me on several cases a few years back. He's still a mutual friend and a golfing buddy."

"So, is he with Mr. Rapp?" Ashley asked.

"Yes, I think he's with him now," Mr. Arlington said.

"We'll get to meet him then, right?" Adam asked.

"No," he said. "On the way to the airport this morning, Mr. Rapp was involved in a car accident. He won't be in Cheyenne anytime soon."

Mrs. Arlington looked at her husband, stunned.

"That poor man," she said. "Will he be okay?"

"Yes, he will, eventually," Mr. Arlington said. "According to the voice mail message, a drunk driver in a truck plowed into his car. He has a broken leg, and it's a pretty bad compound fracture. He'll need surgery on it. He's not going to be able to go anywhere. Apparently, he's getting his own room early this afternoon, and he'll have surgery late today. He should be able to talk to me by tomorrow morning. The message said that Julie Mitchum had been called, too, so she is apparently aware of the situation."

"If Tom has a broken leg and is having surgery to repair a compound fracture, he's probably facing a long rehabilitation," Mrs. Arlington said. "It'd be tough for him to do any good out here, at least not for a long while. I'd imagine the FAA and law enforcement investigations will conclude long before then."

"I see it the same way," Mr. Arlington said. "Now, more than ever, I hope the authorities can put this puzzle together soon."

"Me, too, Dad," Ashley said. "But they have to get a few more pieces of the puzzle first before they can think of putting it together."

"I know, Ash," he said, reaching his hand over his head and behind his seat to squeeze his daughter's hand.

"Should we do anything else?" Mrs. Arlington asked.

"I don't know what we could do," Mr. Arlington said. "We'll offer support however we can and check in with the FAA and then with Tom each day. If Ron is found, he'll need family support though, and we could stand in for Tom. We could be his family till Tom arrives."

"That's true, we can surely do that," his wife said. She turned out of the convenience store parking lot and got on the road that took them to U.S. 191. Just as Adam had mapped out from the Internet, the family headed northeast on State Highway 28, stopping at Sinks Canyon State Park.

"Listen to this," Adam said, reading from a brochure about Sinks Canyon. "It's amazing!"

"Water from the Popo Agie River cascades into a cavern and emerges about a quarter mile away in a large pool," he read. "The river's subterranean course has not been fully explained by geologists."

"That *is* amazing," Ashley commented. "Wouldn't it be fun to go spelunking and discover the river's course?"

"If it was a fun and easy route it would have already been done," said their mother. "Let's be content to look at it from above the ground."

They all laughed.

The Red Canyon vista along State Highway 28 south of Lander was breathtaking. The Arlingtons could see the long, seemingly out-of-place stripes of red rock that had been created when Earth's crust was fractured into massive sheets as tectonic plates collided at the continental divide. The beauty and history of the area were almost enough to take the family's minds off everything that had happened to the Rapps.

"We'll head into Lander, pick up a few things, and then move on to Riverton," Mrs. Arlington said. Everyone nodded in agreement.

As they drove into Lander, Mr. Arlington turned the dial to Wyoming Public Radio. The reporter was saying they had a few more details on the plane crash in Guernsey State Park. The details weren't new to the Arlingtons, however, who had an inside track into the investigation because of their relationship with the Rapps. But they did glean one thing from the report: In addition to the worker, an engineer in the rail yard had also seen the person believed to be Ron Rapp.

After both workers had reported it to the rail yard officer, authorities had been summoned to the area. However, the search turned up no one.

"That's too bad," Adam said. "It's sounds like whoever was in the rail yard just disappeared."

The family pulled out of Lander and headed northeast to Riverton. After Mr. Arlington asked directions on the outskirts of town, the family easily found the bed-and-breakfast where they had reservations.

"This place is beautiful," Ashley said, walking up the steps to the stately old house.

"It's been here for seventy-five years," Mr. Arlington said. "We thought this might be a little different from staying in a hotel, although I know you kids will miss the pool."

"Oh, Dad, we'll manage in a place like this," Adam said with a smile.

After putting their suitcases in their rooms, the family walked around the area, which was outside Riverton's city limits. As they walked, they saw a small airport, which turned out to be the Riverton Regional Airport.

"Maybe they have a shop inside," Ashley said. "It's not even a half-mile from this road to the entrance of the terminal."

"Maybe," Mrs. Arlington said. "Let's see what it's like."

They walked to the terminal and entered. A small coffee shop inside had some rolls that smelled delicious, so the Arlingtons sat down.

"You realize, of course, that this is going to absolutely ruin dinner for us," Mr. Arlington said.

"I do, and I think we should accept the consequences this time," Mrs. Arlington said as everyone laughed. After they ate, they went out in the small area where passengers waited to board the commuter planes that landed at the airport.

Ashley put money in a newspaper machine to get a copy of the *Riverton Ranger,* the local newspaper. Her parents always encouraged her and her brother to read, especially newspapers. On vacation, the local papers gave the family an idea of any special events they could see or visit, in addition to giving Ashley and Adam some perspective on what issues were important to the residents of a particular town. The family would often discuss how those issues related to the issues facing them back home.

Ashley took the paper and let the machine's door close gently. Just then, a man started to put his coins into the machine.

"Sir, you might not want to do that," she said. "I'm sorry, but I got the last paper. If you put your coins in, you won't get anything in return."

"Oh," said the man, a short, stocky fellow in a short-sleeved T-shirt and jeans. "Thanks for letting me know."

As her parents and brother approached her to head back to the bed-and-breakfast, Ashley felt bad about the man not getting a paper.

"Sir," she said, catching his attention as he started to walk away, "if you'd like this paper, you can have it. You have a bag, so it looks like you're catching a plane. I'm staying in Riverton tonight, so I can get a copy later."

"Oh, that's nice of you, but I just wanted it for one thing," said the man, who introduced himself to the Arlingtons as Bill Danier.

"I work for the railroad. When I was coming out of Cheyenne yesterday, I thought I saw a guy hop on my train. I looked when I stopped about a hundred miles later in the mountains, but I couldn't find him. I was afraid he might've been killed—he was being very reckless. Of course, when you hop a train, you're risking your life as well as breaking the law."

"I don't see a story on it," Ashley said, flipping through the pages and holding the paper up so the man could see it.

"Hmm," Danier said. "I'll have to call the office when I get to Cheyenne, because this is odd."

"Odd?" Mrs. Arlington asked. "How so?"

"I never saw the guy again, but a buddy of mine did," Danier said. "An engineer on another train left a message at my house that he had seen a guy jump off my train just south of town. He hopped on another one that was headed north."

"Perhaps he was a transient," Mr. Arlington said.

"Well, that's the strange thing," Danier said. "My friend said this guy had on expensive boots and wore just a black T-shirt and shorts through the mountain pass, which was cold."

"A black T-shirt?" Mr. Arlington asked. He looked at his family and at Bill Danier. "Red hair?"

"Yeah," Danier said. Danier tilted his head sideways and squinted. "Now, how in the world would you know that?"

"Oh my goodness!" Ashley said excitedly. "It must have been Ron!"

"Ron who?" Danier said. "And why would he be hopping our trains? He didn't look like someone we'd usually see copping a free ride."

"He seemed different?" Mrs. Arlington asked.

"He sure did," Danier said. "He was pretty well-groomed, and a lot of people who hop trains aren't really into personal hygiene, much less combing their hair. This guy just seemed out of place. You think you know him?"

"About six feet tall, maybe 175 pounds?" Mrs. Arlington asked.

"Yeah, that sounds about right," Danier said. "The other engineer who saw him was close enough that he could've probably said something to the guy. But then he saw that the guy was in pretty good shape—had some muscles—and he didn't want any trouble. He figured he'd just let him go."

"That man's father is a close friend of mine," Mr. Arlington explained. "The name of the man you saw is Ron Rapp. There are a lot of people looking for him."

"Why?" Danier asked.

"His plane crashed in Guernsey the night before last," Mr. Arlington said. "The plane was brought out in pieces, and not a single piece could've been more than five feet long."

"How awful; it's amazing he's even alive then," Danier said. "But I don't see the link here. Why is he hopping trains?"

"We don't know," Ashley said. "But Ron was last seen at the rail yard just west of Guernsey."

"Trains go in all directions from there," Danier said. "He could have easily hopped one there and eventually ended up on my train."

"This is incredible," Adam said. "I wonder where he's going."

"You keep the paper," Danier said. "That's my plane out there getting ready to leave. It was nice to meet you all. Good luck finding your friend."

After Danier went out to the runway, Mr. Arlington called Julie Mitchum's number.

"Thanks for the lead, Mr. Arlington," Mitchum said after he told her about the encounter with Danier. "You didn't get Mr. Danier's number, did you?"

"No, I didn't," he said. "But his first name is Bill, and like I said, he's an engineer with the railroad."

"Okay, I'll pass along the information and track down a number for Mr. Danier—it shouldn't be too hard to do," she said. "Your help is appreciated. It sounds to me like

Ron is probably long gone from the Riverton area by now—maybe north if Mr. Danier's friend is right. Well, I'll be talking to Tom Rapp after his surgery late this afternoon. You know about that, right?"

"Oh, yes," Mr. Arlington said. "I'll probably call him first thing in the morning."

"Good," Mitchum said. "Please call me if you hear anything else."

"Thanks, I will," he said. "Good-bye."

He relayed his conversation with Julie Mitchum to his family as they walked to a small café where they enjoyed a light supper. Not wanting to walk back through an unfamiliar area when it was dark, the Arlingtons decided to head back to the bed-and-breakfast. As they strode up the steps, the sunset was a spectacular pink with sharp reddish pink clouds illuminating the sky. The Arlingtons sat on the porch enjoying the view and wondering what the next day would bring.

Hot Springs, Hot Trail

The following morning, the Arlingtons went for an early run in the direction opposite the one they had taken to the airport. After coming back for breakfast at the inn, the family headed north out of town.

Passing the Boysen Reservoir, the Arlingtons arrived in Thermopolis, home of the "World's Largest Mineral Hot Springs," according to a sign on the outskirts of town. They checked into a campground just outside town. It had a hookup for electricity, which meant they could run the heater in their tent that night if they needed to, since it didn't stay as warm as their motor home back in Casper.

"We're going to go to the dinosaur museum here," Mrs. Arlington said. "You two want to go?"

"Mom," Adam said, "there are natural hot springs here and a couple of water parks with big slides and everything.

How about we do those today and do the dinosaur thing tomorrow before we leave?"

"How about your mother and I go to the dinosaur museum, and you two take the SUV to the hot springs?" their father asked.

"That works for me," Ashley said with a grin. "Should we drop you off at the museum?"

"No, it's only about three miles from here," he said. "Getting there will be kind of neat, actually. According to the guy here at the campground, there are green footprints painted into the road once you get into downtown Thermopolis. Those shouldn't be too hard to follow to the museum. It's only 9:00 A.M., so we've got all kinds of time. Let's meet back here at the campground at 6:00 for dinner. You two are on your own for lunch."

"Gotcha, Dad," Ashley said. "Got some cash?"

Mr. Arlington pulled out his wallet with a mock sigh and handed over lunch money and water park admission fees to Ashley.

"I suppose you two are saving your money for some spectacular souvenir?" he asked with a grin. Then he and Mrs. Arlington waved them off and headed into town.

Adam and Ashley were excited to visit the water park. When they arrived they were amazed at the strong smell of the sulphur in the water.

"You know what that reminds me of?" Adam asked Ashley as he pinched his nose to keep out the foul air.

"I don't want to know," Ashley said. "Besides, there's nothing wrong with the water, and you'll get used to the smell in a minute."

They changed into their bathing suits and jumped right into the water. After a couple of trips down the slide, they joined in a game of water basketball with a few local high schoolers. Ashley dominated the game and got bored after a while, so she and Adam went back to the slides.

Ashley came down the slide on her stomach, and a lifeguard came over to talk to her.

"You're busted, wild woman," Adam said, grinning at Ashley.

"Oh, I hope not," Ashley answered.

"Are you from around here?" asked the lifeguard, a short young woman who appeared to be in very good shape.

"No, we're just visiting from Washington, D.C.," Ashley said.

"I just noticed that you're pretty good at basketball," said the lifeguard, who introduced herself as Shelly Conrad.

"Thanks," Ashley said. "Do you play?"

"Yes," Shelly said. "I just graduated last year from high school here. I was an all-state point guard, and I'm going to be on the team at the University of Wyoming this fall."

"Good for you—go for it," Ashley said. "I'm going to be a senior at my high school next year. I'm hoping to play college ball, too."

"Are you staying at a motel here in town?" Shelly asked. "We're playing a pick-up game tomorrow night at my high school."

"Oh, we'll be gone by tomorrow night," Ashley said. "We're staying at a campground just outside of town."

"Ooooh, be careful," Shelly said.

"Is it unsafe here?" Ashley asked.

"Not at all—it's usually really safe here," Shelly said. "You didn't hear the talk around town today about the man everyone saw walking around late last night?"

"What man?" Ashley asked.

"Some weird guy, I guess," Shelly said. "It was, like, 3:30 in the morning and pretty cold out, and this guy is walking around in shorts and a black T-shirt. He didn't talk to anyone, and by the time the police were called, they couldn't find him. He supposedly has already left town. Of course, if he hadn't left town, word would've spread pretty fast, so we'd know if he was still here."

"Oh, my goodness," Ashley said. "Do you know if he had red hair?"

"I don't know; let me ask my friend," Shelly said. She turned to another girl about her age and said, "Hey, Cathy, that guy everyone saw last night—red hair?"

Cathy nodded her head yes and then made a muscle with her arm, adding, "Yep, red hair, and from the story I heard, he's got muscles."

"It's him," Adam said. "Ron Rapp was here!"

Adam and Ashley got out of the water, showered, and headed to the lobby of the water park. They got directions to the dinosaur museum and drove over right away.

Their parents weren't there, so they traced the route back to the campground. Still they could find no sign of their parents. That wasn't unusual because Mr. and Mrs. Arlington loved to shop in downtown areas wherever they went. There was no telling where they could be—out walking in the country or perhaps at a bookstore or coffee shop downtown.

"Let's go looking for Ron," Ashley said to Adam as they climbed back into the SUV. "It's not even noon yet, and from what we know, he doesn't have a car. Unless he hopped another train or hitchhiked, he's got to be near here."

"Okay, but can we go through a drive-through and get some food to take with us?" Adam said.

"Oh, yeah, of course we can," Ashley said. "I'm hungry, too."

They quickly found a drive-through and ordered burgers, fries, and drinks. As they waited to pay and pick up their food, they talked about their next step.

"Where do you think Ron could be headed?" Ashley asked.

"I don't know," Adam answered. "They found his wallet in the plane, so he probably doesn't have any credit cards with him. All he'd have is any cash that was in his pockets—at least that's my guess."

"Sounds reasonable," Ashley said. "Call up your on-line map."

Adam turned on his laptop computer and pulled up a map of the area.

"I'd guess Ron's going north because, for whatever reason, that's what he's done twice to get here," Adam said. "East would be my second guess because I'm sure all his stuff is back at his house or apartment near Devils Tower. But there's no major road east out of Thermopolis."

"What are the ways out of here to the north?" Ashley asked.

"There are two possibilities. U.S. 20 and then 16 would put him on I-90 at Buffalo. From there he could go straight to U.S. 14, which gives him a straight shot to Devils Tower and his home."

"What's the second possibility?" Ashley asked.

"He could take State Highway 120 northwest," Adam said. "But except for the city of Meeteetse, there's nothing for 117 miles until Cody."

"You don't think he'd take that route then?" Ashley asked.

"Good question," Adam said. "I don't really know. I have no idea what Ron is doing, where he's going, or what he's thinking. If he's trying to get home to the Devils Tower area, then I definitely think he's going the I-90 way. But if he's trying to run away or avoid the people looking for him, he might be headed for Cody. Anyone going to Yellowstone National Park would head toward Cody because Cody is due east of Yellowstone on U.S. 14/16. A person could really drop out of sight in a place like that!"

They decided to head out of town on U.S. 20 and go just north of Thermopolis to the towns of Kirby and Lucerne.

"In those small towns," Ashley said, "people see everything that happens. If he was in a vehicle that passed through either of those two towns, we'll know about it."

"We won't if we don't stop for gas first," Adam said, pointing at the gas gauge needle. "Remember what Mom told us before we took our driver's tests: 'E does not mean Enough.'"

The two laughed at the memory, and Ashley pulled over. This time it was Adam's turn to pump the gas. Since the SUV had been driven a couple of hundred miles in hot weather, the essentials under the hood needed to be checked; Ashley would handle that.

Adam had only $10, so Ashley went in with him to pay for the gas. They looked around the convenience store and grabbed some bottled water, just in case they became thirsty. As they went to pay for it, they noticed a sale rack with gray sweatshirts for only $5 that said "Wyoming" on the front in brown letters. The front of a buffalo decorated the area under the letters, and its backside and tail were on the back of the shirts.

"These are great," Ashley said to Adam, "but like Dad said, I have some other souvenirs in mind on this trip. Guess I won't get one right now. Maybe we'll run into them later though, and I'll see if I have any money left."

"Maybe," said Adam. "I don't think I'll get one now either."

"I thought once those were marked down, they'd go like hotcakes," the cashier said.

"Well, it is pretty warm out for sweatshirts," Ashley said to the man. "Maybe the buffalo is scaring people off," she added, grinning.

He laughed, too. "Maybe, but I did sell one of them," the man said. "There was a guy who walked in here from town. Just walked here—no car, no truck, no nothing. This isn't the kind of area that people walk to either—we're pretty isolated. This guy was just, like, on his own."

"Red hair, black T-shirt, right?" Ashley asked, looking at Adam as they both realized it sounded like Ron Rapp.

"Yes, do you know him?" the man asked.

"We do," Ashley said. "Did he say anything?"

"Not a single word," the man said. "He wasn't rude or anything, but he just sort of smiled uncomfortably when I asked him where he came from. He looked a little weathered; like he hadn't shaved in a couple of days and maybe hadn't bathed, either. Just kind of odd, you know what I mean?"

"So he didn't say where he was headed?" Adam asked.

"I asked him that exact question," the cashier said. "But he didn't answer. He just kind of tilted his head sideways at me. That's when I noticed it."

"What do you mean by 'it'? What did you notice?" Ashley asked.

"He had a little bit of blood coming out of his ear," the cashier said. "I wanted to say something to him about it, but at that point I got a little nervous. He had a lot of muscle, and I couldn't have handled him if he took offense at my curiosity. I don't mean to be rude, but he looked like a tough guy in rough shape. You two kids better be careful about catching up with him—maybe your friend isn't in the mood just now to be friendly . . ."

Ashley briefly explained to the man about the crash and how Ron Rapp, the pilot, had been sighted afterward but not found.

"I heard about that crash on the news!" the cashier exclaimed. "I feel awful about this. I should have offered to help the guy or call 911 when I saw that he was bleeding from the ear. But I never connected him with the accident. I didn't think about him having a head injury. He just acted so odd, I figured his injury was probably from a fight, and I didn't want to get in on it. No wonder you two want to find him. I hope you do!"

"He couldn't have gotten far when he left here," Ashley said. "You said this isn't the kind of place where people travel on foot. How long ago was he here?"

"Maybe an hour," the man answered.

An hour! Adam and Ashley thought.

"We just missed him!" Adam said. "We'll head north; maybe we can catch him."

"Wait a minute, don't go running off yet," the cashier said. "Someone in a white pickup gave him a ride in the parking lot. I think they were highway construction workers because they had one of those big pickups with four doors, and your friend got in the back. The three guys in it looked like pretty nice guys. They were wearing those orange vests that construction workers always have on. I had other customers in the store, so I didn't see which way they went."

"Do you know if there is any construction going on around here?" Adam asked.

"None I can think of," the cashier said. "If you'd have asked me last summer, I could've pointed in any direction, and you could've found construction blocking the highway."

"Well, thanks for your help," Ashley said, getting her change back for the gas and water.

As Adam and Ashley headed for the door, the man came out from behind the counter.

"Hey, wait a minute!" the man said, catching Ashley as she opened the door for Adam. The man reached out toward the rack and took two sweatshirts off hangers. "A couple of larges. Here, take them, they're on the house. You two kids sure are nice, and I hope you find your pilot friend. Enjoy them and think nice thoughts of Wyoming whenever you wear them."

"Oh, sir," Adam said, "that's nice, but our parents really wouldn't let us accept . . ."

"I insist," the cashier said. "I own the place, so I reserve the right to hand out a few smiles every now and then.

It'll make up some for how I let your friend go when I really should have been more concerned about his injury."

"That's very kind of you," Ashley said. "We will enjoy them and think of our vacation here when we wear them."

Ashley got behind the wheel of the SUV, and Adam turned his computer on.

"I downloaded the highway construction report the night before last," Adam said. "There's work on I-25 near Cheyenne, but that wouldn't affect us. Some on I-90, too, but workers doing stuff over there wouldn't be over here in the middle of the day. Hey, look at this! There's a big construction project just outside of Cody on the way to Yellowstone!"

"Here we go," Ashley said.

"To Yellowstone?" Adam asked.

"No, just to Cody. It's about two hours from here," Ashley said. "It's just past noon, so we have six hours before we have to be back to the campground for dinner with Mom and Dad. What do you say?"

"Cody, here we come!" Adam exclaimed.

They made good time on the way to Cody. As they came to the Meeteetse exit, they saw a white four-door pickup with a State Highway logo on the side pulled over at the end of the off-ramp. Ashley pulled alongside it, and Adam rolled down his window when he saw two highway workers inside.

"Hi, sir," Adam said to the driver. "Could I ask you a question?"

"Sure," the driver answered. "What is it?"

"Is there another vehicle like yours that headed out of Thermopolis in the past two hours or so?" Adam asked.

"Sure, probably two or three more," the driver said. "We're bringing up some supplies. We're just taking our lunch break, then we all head to the big project just outside of Cody."

"You wouldn't happen to have a radio in there to contact the other State Highway vehicles, would you?" Adam asked.

"No, we don't," the man said. "But we do have cell phones. Why, what's going on?"

Adam quickly recapped the crash and the strange journey Ron Rapp seemed to be taking. He also mentioned the convenience store cashier in Thermopolis who said he saw Ron get into a State Highway department vehicle, and that Ron might be bleeding from one ear, possibly an injury from the plane crash.

"I heard about that crash and the manhunt for the pilot," the man said. "It's big news around here, a real mystery. From what you say, the guy sounds like he could be in serious condition, if it *is* the pilot that hitched a ride. Let me call and see what we can find out."

The man went down a list of various ID numbers for the vehicles and their accompanying cell phone numbers. He asked the other worker in the car to help him figure out which other trucks had gone to Thermopolis. The driver, who said his name was Jeff Harris, called one, but the worker who answered said he hadn't picked up a rider.

Jeff called a second truck. That driver, likewise, had not picked up anyone. However, he told Jeff that another driver who had also gone to Thermopolis mentioned that he had picked up someone. Jeff asked for that truck's number and dialed.

"This is Jeff Harris," he said into the cell phone. "I under-stand you picked up someone when you gassed up in Ther-mopolis. I've got some of his friends right here, and they're looking for him—they say it's pretty important. What's that? . . . Okay, thanks. Good-bye."

"What did he say?" Adam asked.

"They did pick up your pilot friend," Jeff said. "He appar-ently didn't say a word the whole trip. They let him off in Cody. I guess he collapsed against the side of the car for a minute. They didn't smell alcohol or anything on him, though. The highway workers thought he was sick. They tried to help him, but he took off running on the main street in Cody right where it picks up when you exit the highway, about fifteen minutes ago. He was in good shape—outdistanced them easily. They're already back on the job west of Cody now. I hope your friend is okay. It sounds like he needs some help."

"Thank you very much," Ashley said. She pulled the vehicle up to the ramp but didn't merge back onto the highway right away as Adam had expected her to.

"What's going on, Ash?" Adam asked. "Aren't we going to Cody?"

"I'm not sure," she said. "Let's stop and call Julie Mitchum and let her know what's going on. Dad left her number right here in the car. We're still a little way from Cody, and Ron will have a head start on us as it is."

They called Julie Mitchum on their cell phone, but she wasn't there. However, Ashley had her paged, and after a short delay, she came to the phone. Ashley told her every-thing that had happened. She also told her about the Wyoming sweatshirt Ron was wearing.

"Okay, Ashley, thanks," Mitchum said. "I'll call the police and rescue folks in Cody. We talked to seven of Ron's closest friends in northeastern Wyoming, to his father, and to two buddies from college who Ron stays in touch with. And we haven't a single clue relating to any possible criminal activity Ron is either involved in or running from. At least he finally has some warm clothes on. I'm sure sleeping in that T-shirt out in the cold hasn't done him any good. Let us know if you hear anything else. Good-bye."

Ashley hung up the phone and told Adam what Julie Mitchum had said.

"Let's go ahead and drive to Cody," Ashley said, "even if it is just for a little while."

"Okay, if you think that's the best thing to do," Adam said.

"What do you mean?" Ashley asked. "Do you think we should head back to the campground in Thermopolis right now?"

"No, we can go have a quick look in Cody," Adam said. "It would just be better if Mom and Dad were with us and if we hadn't gotten all set up at the campground in Thermopolis already. Then, we could have set up in Cody."

"Good idea," Ashley said, starting the SUV again. But instead of heading north, she turned south on State Highway 20.

"What do you mean good idea?" Adam asked. "And this isn't the way to Cody."

"Oh, yes, it is," Ashley said.

"I don't understand," Adam said.

"Adam, you hit the nail right on the head," Ashley said. "We have to get Mom and Dad and get the tent packed. We could be in Cody before it gets dark if we hurry."

Adam grinned. "Hey, you're right; that *was* a good idea I had. I just didn't know it."

During the eighty-minute drive back to the campground in Thermopolis, Adam and Ashley tried to put together the pieces of the puzzle they had just gathered.

"First of all," Adam said, calling up the map of Wyoming on his Internet atlas, "Ron has gone a lot of miles in a short period of time. It's almost like he's on the run from something. But what?"

"That's a hard question," Ashley said. "Maybe there isn't an answer to it."

"I don't follow you on that one, Ash. How can there not be an answer? And we still have no clue about the crash itself."

"What I'm saying, Adam, is that maybe when we get an answer to the crash itself, the answers to other questions will also fall in line. Remember what Julie Mitchum told us? Investigators have talked to the ten people who know Ron the best. Not a single one of them can pinpoint anything that would lead investigators to believe Ron is involved in drugs, or that he committed some sort of crime. Maybe the reason he's running lies in the crash itself."

"I also wonder how serious Ron's injuries are," Adam said. "It sounds bad, really bad."

"Yeah," Ashley agreed. "I have to think that if he wasn't in such good shape before the crash he might not have made it to this point."

"Still, Ash," Adam said, "although we've been assuming that this man is Ron, you have to admit that it is practically impossible that anyone survived that crash. The plane just plowed into that hill. It'd be like hitting a brick wall."

"I'm still wrestling with that one," Ashley said. "Of all the questions, the one about the actual crash is the toughest. But, like I said, I think once we have the answer to that one, we'll be able to put the other pieces of the puzzle together to see a picture of what really happened."

The pair made good time getting back to Thermopolis. When they reached the campground, they saw their parents sitting outside the tent.

"Well, hello, you two," Mrs. Arlington said as she saw Adam and Ashley get out of the SUV. "You're back early."

"So are you and Dad," Ashley said.

"We're just resting for a few minutes; then we're going to head to the downtown area, have coffee, and go to a bookstore," Mrs. Arlington said.

"Can we put that on hold?" Ashley asked. "We've got some big news about Ron. He's been seen, and he can't be far from here."

"You're kidding!" their father said.

Ashley told her parents what had happened, and Adam filled in a few of the blanks when she was done. After their parents asked them a few questions, everyone agreed to break camp immediately and hit the road toward Cody—and hopefully toward Ron.

Close Encounter

The Arlingtons arrived in Cody at about 4:00, so there was plenty of sunshine left in the day. They stopped at the local police department, where a state patrolman was already talking with the Cody police and a county deputy about the mysterious and unpredictable Ron Rapp.

Mrs. Arlington introduced herself and her family to all three law enforcement officers. However, although they had Adam's description of Ron, the police had not been able to pick up his trail in Cody. The Arlingtons thanked the police for their time and then drove around town. Cody, named after William F. "Buffalo Bill" Cody, was the last big outpost before the east entrance to Yellowstone.

As they headed down the main street in town, they saw a major chain discount store. Mr. Arlington pulled into the parking lot, and the family got out of the vehicle. "We need to stop in here and replace that sleeping bag Adam ripped this morning," Mr. Arlington told his wife.

"I didn't mean to rip it," Adam said to his mom. "The zipper on the tent snagged the bag when we were packing up."

"I'm sure it was an accident, son, but that material was waterproof and the bag won't stay warm or dry in bad weather now," said Mr. Arlington. "We've gotten a lot of hard use out of it anyway with all the camping we've done. Now is as good a time as any to replace it and to pick up a few other things we need."

A brisk wind was blowing through the parking lot as the sun went behind the clouds.

"You may need a warm sleeping bag in good condition tonight, Adam, if this chill continues," Mrs. Arlington said. "The temperature can really drop here at night. It's starting already. I'm putting on a light jacket."

"I have a sweatshirt in the back," Mr. Arlington added. The colder weather was the perfect opportunity for Ashley and Adam to wear their complimentary "WYOMING" sweatshirts.

"Those look warm," their dad said. "Where did you get them?"

Adam and Ashley told the story about how the convenience store owner in Thermopolis had given them the sweatshirts and also sold one to Ron.

"You know, we aren't really sure where to start looking for Ron, or what to do," Mr. Arlington said as they entered the discount store. "I'll call Mr. Rapp. You all can go back to the sporting goods department and get a new sleeping bag. We also need another container or two of propane for the stove and the camping lanterns if we're going to be camping tonight."

"Okay," Mrs. Arlington said. "If you get off the phone first, meet us back in sporting goods. If we get done first, we'll catch up with you here. If we miss each other, let's just meet in the store's snack bar."

"Mom, can I head back to electronics and see if they have a program I need?" Adam asked.

"And can I go over to the book section to see if they have a book on all the historical spots in Wyoming?" Ashley asked.

Mrs. Arlington agreed and went to the sporting goods department alone. As she went through the various shelves of outdoor equipment, she easily found the propane. But she couldn't find the right kind of sleeping bag. All the sleeping bags the Arlingtons used were good for temperatures below freezing. The ones Mrs. Arlington saw displayed were only good just above freezing temperatures.

From where she stood, Mrs. Arlington could see a man wearing a store vest walking toward the cash register in the sporting goods department. She heard another worker already behind the counter ask a customer if that customer had a bill "any smaller than that." From where she was standing, she couldn't tell if there was a long line at the register, but it sounded like there was. She never heard an answer about whether the customer had a smaller bill.

"Oh well," she thought to herself with a smile. "I'll just pay with a credit card since that large bill will probably clean out the register."

The worker she had seen a moment ago came out from behind the register and within view.

"Sir," she motioned, "could I have some help over here, please?"

"Sure, but could you please wait just a second?" the young man asked. "We're just swamped."

"No problem," she said. She looked around some more and picked up a couple of other things for the rest of the trip.

"How can I help you?" the store worker came over a few minutes later and asked.

"I need a sleeping bag rated for temperatures below freezing. Of all these on display, I don't see any like that," Mrs. Arlington said.

"We do have them," the worker said. "They're just up higher. Here, I'll get a ladder and get down a couple to show you."

The store worker, who wore a name tag that said "Jaime," got down two boxes that each had a sleeping bag inside. Mrs. Arlington looked at the temperatures rated on the boxes.

"Perfect," she said. "Just what I'm looking for. I'll take this one."

"If you follow me around the corner, I'll ring you up," Jaime said.

"And I can pay with small bills or my credit card," she said with a smile.

"Man, we had about five other people in line when that guy pulled out the $100 bill," Jaime said. "It wasn't that bad, because he was buying a sleeping bag and a small tent. But usually on the bigger-ticket items people pay by check or charge. We were just getting rushed, and this customer wouldn't answer my coworker's question. He wasn't confrontational or anything, he just didn't seem to want to speak."

"Odd," Mrs. Arlington said. "I hope he's all right."

"He's out of my department now," Jaime said grinning. "So in my book now he's okay."

Mrs. Arlington suddenly remembered that the convenience store cashier in Thermopolis had told Adam and Ashley earlier that Ron had not spoken at all when buying his sweatshirt. She was just going to ask Jaime what this silent customer with the $100 bill had looked like when Ashley and Adam arrived at the register. She turned to them.

"No luck?" she asked the kids.

"None for me, but I saw another place when we were driving here that I think might have it," Adam said.

"I had plenty of luck," Ashley said, setting a book on the register. "They had two books, and this one cost less than the other one, but has just as much information and more pictures. Can you buy it, Mom, and I'll pay you back?"

"How about when you're done, you let us all look at it," her mom said. "I'll pay for it, and you won't have to pay me back. Deal?"

"Sure," Ashley said. "Thanks a lot, Mom."

Jaime scanned the prices and Mrs. Arlington handed him her credit card. Before she could ask him about the "odd" customer, he looked at Ashley and Adam and smiled.

"Nice sweatshirts," Jaime said.

"Thanks," Adam said.

"I've seen a lot of Wyoming sweatshirts," Jaime said. "But until today I'd never seen one like that with the brown lettering and the buffalo on the front and back. Those are cool. And counting the two you are wearing, I've seen three in the last few minutes."

"You saw another one?" Ashley asked.

"Yes." He looked at Mrs. Arlington and added, "Remember the man you heard my coworker talking to, the man who had the $100 bill but was in a daze and didn't answer our questions? He was wearing the exact same sweatshirt."

"It had to be Ron!" Ashley said excitedly. "Red hair, stubbly whiskers?" she asked.

"Exactly," Jaime said. "I don't know his name, because, like I said, he paid with cash. But that's what he looked like, and he was wearing the same sort of sweatshirt you two are wearing."

"Which way did he go?" Ashley asked.

"I don't know; I went to help your mom find the sleeping bag after that," Jaime said. "He might have left the store. But it was only about five minutes ago, so maybe he's still here."

"Thanks," Mrs. Arlington said, hurriedly stuffing the receipt in one of their bags and handing them to Adam to carry.

"Let's split up," she said. "Adam, you go toward the front of the store. Ashley, you go toward the back. And I'll go down the middle the way I came in."

"Okay," Ashley said. "And we'll meet at the snack bar."

They started looking and saw each other several times but found no sign of Ron. They found Mr. Arlington waiting in the snack bar and briefed him on what had just happened.

"He can't be far," Mr. Arlington said. "Let's carefully check the parking lot. Ashley, you and I will take the west side.

Anne and Adam, you two take the east side. I'll call the police. We'll meet at the SUV in ten minutes."

They ran out to the parking lot, slowing down as they left the sidewalk because several cars were turning in the cramped drop-off area. Again, what appeared to be a sizzling trail cooled considerably. There was no sign of Ron in the parking lot. The Arlingtons met back at the SUV and got inside, mainly to get out of the chilly wind.

"At least we know Ron bought a tent and sleeping bag— that's what the clerk told me before Adam and Ashley met me," Mrs. Arlington said. "So he's obviously sleeping outside. And he has at least a little bit of money because the store clerk said he paid with a $100 bill."

"I need to call Tom and then Julie Mitchum," Mr. Arlington said. "Tom really needs to know for sure that Ron is still alive. I'll let Julie know, too."

A police car arrived in the parking lot as he began to dial the cell phone. Mrs. Arlington, Adam, and Ashley got out of the SUV and went to talk to the officers.

"Hi, Tom, it's Alex again," Mr. Arlington said. "Good news: Ron was just seen at a store here in Cody about ten minutes ago."

"That's great; did he look okay?"

"I guess so," Mr. Arlington replied. "He bought a tent and sleeping bag, so he's obviously going to be warm. I think that's a good sign."

"Good," Mr. Rapp said.

"Tom, my family and I are going to put our heads together and try to find him. It looks like he might be headed toward Yellowstone National Park, though we're not sure why."

"Yellowstone—that might make sense," Mr. Rapp said.

"How's that?" Mr. Arlington asked.

"We went to Yellowstone several times when he was a child—Ron, his mother, and I. We kept going, three out of four years in a row, until we moved back East. Ron was always saying he was going to live in Yellowstone when he grew up. We told him he could live near there, but he couldn't live in Yellowstone itself because it's a national park. Actually, he always talked about being a park ranger. When he first got the job at Devils Tower last year I reminded him of what he had said about being a ranger when he grew up."

"That's good to know; maybe we're on the right track at this point," Mr. Arlington said. "I still have to call Julie Mitchum, so I should go. I just wanted to update you."

"That's great, Alex. Call if you find out anything at all. And thanks."

"You're welcome—and start getting that leg healed up so we can golf again," Mr. Arlington said. "Good-bye."

He then dialed Julie Mitchum and told her what had happened in Cody just ten minutes earlier, in addition to passing on the information about what Ron was now wearing.

"Great," Mitchum said. "Those stores have good security cameras everywhere, so I'll ask the police to get a copy of the tape for the past hour and send it to me as soon as possible. And I'd like to send a copy to Ron's father. Hopefully he can confirm that this man really is Ron."

"Great plan," Mr. Arlington said. "I just talked to Tom, and I know he's living for our phone calls. If you could call and tell him about the security tape, he'd be grateful. We'll talk to you soon."

"All right; it sounds like we might really have something to go on. Thanks for calling."

Mr. Arlington hung up the phone and waited for the rest of his family to finish talking to the police. After a few minutes they returned to the car. "It sounds like Ron wants to get lost where no one can find him," he said, prompting Ashley to open the atlas. "Where would you go if you didn't want to be found?"

"Wyoming," Adam said with a smile. "Just about anywhere in Wyoming."

As they all looked at the map, Mr. Arlington told the others what Ron's father had said about Yellowstone.

"Yellowstone, h-m-m," Ashley said. "A bunch of travelers, not a lot of locals—no one would draw attention to themselves by being there, and there aren't a lot of people who would notice him, not like they would if he went to a small town or a little campground. He *has* to be hiking to Yellowstone."

Mr. Arlington put the vehicle in reverse and carefully looked over each of his shoulders before backing up. "Buckle up everyone," he said. "We're heading to Yellowstone."

On the Brink
of a Breakthrough

The Arlingtons drove east on U.S. 14/16 toward Yellowstone, going through the scenic Shoshone National Forest and its towering pine trees.

There was also plenty of prairie in the area. They entered the park and saw buffalo almost immediately.

"Wow," Adam said. "What majestic animals."

"Majestic—that's a really good word to describe buffalo," his mother said.

They also saw Yellowstone Lake to the south. At that point, they were faced with a decision.

"It's that time," Mr. Arlington said. "We're looking for a needle in a haystack."

"So, what we really need," Ashley said, "is a metal detector."

"Actually," Mrs. Arlington said, "that's a good approach to take."

"A metal detector?" Ashley asked.

"No," her mother said. "But we want to deduce where the needle is likely to be at this point. We need to try and think like Ron might be thinking right now."

"That's going to be tough. He hasn't tried to call his dad or any of his friends. He hasn't done anything logical since the crash. How can we know how he thinks?" Adam asked.

"Remember, Adam, you wondered before if Ron had amnesia or something because he's been acting so oddly since the crash?" Mrs. Arlington said. "Maybe he really does have some sort of head injury that has dazed or confused him. If he really doesn't remember who he is, it's harder on the one hand and easier on the other," she continued. "He would have few or no preconceived notions, at least none that we know of."

"I see," Ashley said. "He doesn't know or recognize anyone, and might not know where he's going, but he still has to survive. It's almost like he's alone in a foreign country."

"That's my guess, too," Mrs. Arlington said. "So, what would you do if you didn't know anyone and were in a foreign country?"

"I'd look for anything that looks even vaguely familiar. And I'd want it to be somewhere I wouldn't stand out— where I could keep a low profile. There'd have to be water nearby to survive," Adam said, "and there would have to be trees nearby as well because I'd want some cover."

"In Yellowstone," Mr. Arlington said, "Ron can find trees anywhere. Let's look at a map and study his options."

"North to Tower Falls, or south to West Thumb and then to the geyser basin where Old Faithful is," Adam reported.

"There's water in both directions," Ashley said, looking at her brother's computer map while her parents looked at an atlas. "But in my eyes, there's only one place to go because he'll probably need to fish for food and have water close by."

"I'm thinking Yellowstone Lake," Adam said. "And you, Ash?"

"Same thing," she answered.

"Okay," said their father. "We'll go along with that guess, too. Looks like I need to take a left up here."

They headed toward Yellowstone Lake and saw more buffalo at the side of the road. At another bend, they saw a park ranger standing outside his truck. Mr. Arlington pulled up behind the ranger's vehicle, put on his hazard lights, and stopped. The ranger came over to the SUV.

"Are you folks lost?" asked the ranger, who had the last name "Matthews" on his uniform name tag.

"No," Mr. Arlington said. "We're just wondering where someone would go if they just had a tent and a sleeping bag."

"It depends where they parked their car, or if they had a camper," Matthews said.

"No car and no camper," Mr. Arlington said. "What if he was just on foot?"

"Then he couldn't have gotten into the park," Matthews said.

"Maybe he came into the park in someone else's vehicle and then hopped out when he got where he wanted to go," Mr. Arlington said.

"That's quite a hypothesis," the ranger said. "We have a lot of really remote areas where someone could camp unseen for quite a while. But if this person is alone and looking for a place close by with water—which I'd assume he'd need since without a vehicle he'd have no access to any of the campgrounds within the park—I'd guess Yellowstone Lake. But you have to camp within the designated campgrounds here. You can't just pitch a tent anywhere. If you did that and got caught, you'd be asked to move your tent and get a camping permit, or to leave the park. You'd have to be pretty well hidden to pull it off down by the lake."

"Okay," Mr. Arlington said. "That's what we're suspecting, too."

"Is this something that I need to be aware of?" the ranger asked.

"Actually, we're looking for a park ranger, a friend whose airplane crashed on the opposite corner of the state from here," Mr. Arlington replied.

"Oh, yeah, I heard about that guy, Rapp, wasn't it? A guide from Devils Tower?" Matthews said. "You think he's up here? The last I heard about it from my supervisor, he was somewhere around Riverton and no one knew what he was up to or if he was injured."

"He was seen in Cody today," Mr. Arlington said. "You'll probably hear about it the next time you check in. I'm very good friends with his father, and we're trying to help."

"Well, sir, just be careful and be smart," Matthews said. "And if you need any help, call on us. We'll do all we can to help him if he needs it."

"Will do," Mr. Arlington said. "Thank you very much."

"Have a good day," Matthews said, tipping his hat toward the Arlingtons and then heading back toward his pickup.

The Arlingtons kept traveling as close to the lakeshore as possible. Several times they got out when they thought they saw a tent. One time, they did actually see a tent, but it was just a family using it for relief from the sunshine as they ate. As the Arlingtons turned a corner to head toward West Thumb, Ashley thought she saw a tent down by the lake.

Mr. Arlington pulled the SUV over, and the family carefully crossed the road together.

"Let's stay close to each other," said Mr. Arlington. "If that is a tent and Ron is inside, he may not recognize us. We might spook him."

They headed down to where Ashley thought she had seen the tent. But it turned out to be just a torn piece of tablecloth held up by two branches.

"It sure did look like a tent, at least until we got closer," Adam said.

"Good guess, Ash," her mom said. "We should probably go get it and put it in a trash can."

"I'll do it," Ashley said. "It's only about thirty yards from here, right on the water."

"I'll go with her," Adam said. "Besides, I want to feel the water to see if it's cold."

Mr. and Mrs. Arlington gazed out across the crystal blue lake as Adam and Ashley went down to retrieve the tablecloth. Their parents lost sight of them for a moment as they passed through a few trees but picked them up again as they neared the blowing cloth.

As Ashley pulled the cloth down, Adam went down to the water. He felt it and was surprised to find it so cold. He dried his hand on his pant leg and looked at the lake.

"I've got it, Adam," Ashley said, standing about fifteen feet up from the shore. "Let's go back now."

"All right," Adam said. He turned and started to head back up. Just then he heard a rustling noise in a group of trees about twenty yards away. He looked closer and saw something sort of shiny, like vinyl. He took a few steps closer as Ashley came down next to him.

"Oh, look!" Adam said. "Ashley, hidden over in that cluster of trees and long grass—it is a tent!"

Knowing better than to approach the tent alone, Ashley and Adam thought fast and ran back up the slope to where their parents were, rather than yelling for them to come down and alerting whoever was in the tent.

"Should we call the police or the park rangers?" Adam asked. "Or go down there?"

"Let's carefully go down there, just to see what we can see," their dad said. "If it is Ron, we don't want him to slip away again. If it's not him, we don't want to have called the police for nothing on whoever is there."

Mr. and Mrs. Arlington walked slowly as Ashley and Adam followed. They approached the tent from the shore side. They could hear the wind blowing back the flap of the rain cover, which hadn't been fastened to the side. It was a small tent, just like the kind the man at the store in Cody had described selling to Ron.

"I can't see anything inside it yet," Mr. Arlington whispered to the group. "Let's just act like we're casually walking along the shore, but be very quiet. It looks like the front zipper entrance of the tent is facing the water, so we'll be able to get a good look."

They walked in front of the tent and could see through the zipped mesh entrance that no one was inside. They saw a lone sleeping bag. On top of the sleeping bag was the same sort of guide book that Ashley had picked up in Cody.

"I'm going to take a quick look," Mr. Arlington said. "Keep a good lookout while I see if there's anything else in there."

Ashley looked to the north, Adam to the south, and Mrs. Arlington to the west. Mr. Arlington unzipped the tent, which appeared to be brand-new, and examined the sleeping bag, which also seemed to be just out of the box. He picked up the guide book carefully because it was open, and he didn't want to lose the reader's page.

"This is a map of Yellowstone," he said. "There's a circle around the geyser basin."

"That's where Old Faithful is," his wife replied as he left everything the way it was and zipped the tent. "How far are we from there?"

"Maybe fifteen miles at the most," he said. "Let's go."

The family ran back to the SUV and headed toward the west side of the park and the geyser basin. They were all a little nervous during the ride, sensing that they were on the brink of something important. On top of that, no one knew how Ron would react if, or when, they found him. That fact was not lost on either of the older Arlingtons.

"You know, maybe we should call the park rangers or law enforcement right now," Mr. Arlington said. "What if Ron panics when we approach him?"

"Oh, Dad, please don't," Adam said. "He'd rather see a familiar face than someone with a gun or in a uniform. Then he might really freak out."

"He may not even recognize us," Mrs. Arlington pointed out.

"But if the rangers or police spook him and he escapes us again," Ashley said, "we might never find him. Don't forget, he might be a little incapacitated mentally right now, but he's still had ranger training, and he's in good shape physically. We're too close to let him slip away again."

"That's a good point," her mother agreed. "How about this: We won't call the rangers on the way there, but if we see Ron at the geyser basin, we'll let the rangers know what's going on."

"Okay with me," Adam said.

"Me, too," Ashley concurred.

The Arlingtons saw more and more wildlife as they drove toward the geyser basin. Next to the damage still readily apparent from the fire at the park in the 1980s—burned trees still lined the road more than a decade later—the buffalo and other animals were the most spectacular sights at the park.

"If you think this is neat, wait until the geyser basin," Mrs. Arlington said to Adam and Ashley.

As they passed a sign that said the next turn would take them to Old Faithful, Adam and Ashley looked at each other, wrinkling their noses.

"That smell," Adam said. "It's very familiar."

"I remember it," Ashley said. "It's just like the smell at the hot springs in Thermopolis."

"Yes, that's right," their mom said. "It's the same sulphur you smelled. That's what all these geysers are, too—hot springs."

They kept scanning the roads for any sign of Ron as they pulled into the parking lot of Old Faithful. Hundreds of people were already there.

"Speaking of a needle in a haystack," Adam said, "I'd like our chances better if that was all we were looking for."

"No kidding," Ashley said. "Look at all these people."

"Well, we can look around the area while we're keeping an eye out for Ron," Mr. Arlington said. "There's a lot to see here besides Old Faithful, although Old Faithful is by far the most impressive thing."

"What else is there?" Adam asked.

"There's a walkway that goes all the way around this area past geyser after geyser," Mrs. Arlington noted from a park brochure they had picked up at the entrance. "Some are bigger than others, and some are more spectacular than others. It's just a big collection of geysers that happen to be in the same place—a real collection of Mother Nature's."

After learning that Old Faithful wasn't supposed to give its impressive shower for another hour, the Arlingtons followed the wooden walkways and admired the other geysers. They saw no sign of Ron Rapp.

"Look, someone threw some coins in that one," Adam said. "Do you have any change, Mom?"

"Someone did throw coins in there, but you are definitely *not* supposed to throw anything into the geysers," his mom warned.

"I didn't know that," Adam said. "Why would people do it then?"

"Either out of ignorance or else out of a disrespect for nature," Mr. Arlington said. "It's too bad because places like this are so important."

They finished their walkway tour and went over to Old Faithful to wait for its next water show. They sat down and watched chipmunks dart out from under the wooden benches, creating a sort of outside theater in which Old Faithful could work its magic. Since it was late in the afternoon and the big display was still at least thirty minutes away, the crowd had yet to really gather.

"Can I go to the visitor center?" Adam asked.

"Yeah, and can I go with him?" Ashley chipped in.

"Sure, we'll be right here, but don't take too long," Mr. Arlington said. "We're not going to stay another hour and a quarter after this eruption just to see another."

"Gotcha, Dad," Ashley said, and she and Adam walked toward the visitor center, which was not far from where their parents were sitting. Ashley and Adam read some of the information displays in the center. After a while, Ashley wanted to pick up some pamphlets, while Adam wanted to look for postcards to send to his friends.

"If we get split up, let's just meet back where Mom and Dad are sitting," Ashley said as the crowd grew within the visitor center.

"Okay," Adam agreed. As he looked for the postcards, the crowd grew bigger by the minute. By the time he looked around to see if Ashley was still in the building, there were people everywhere. Adam went outside and was shocked to see that the crowd seemed to have grown exponentially as the time for Old Faithful's eruption drew near.

"Oh, well," Adam thought to himself as he looked toward the seats, which were all full. "I bet Mom and Dad saved me and Ash seats."

Adam thought about going to his right as he came out of the shop to get ice cream for his family, but the lines were too long. He shook off that idea but gazed to the right anyway, toward the end of the seating. There, with his back to Adam, sat a man with red hair and a gray sweatshirt sporting a buffalo's back.

Approaching carefully so as not to scare him off, Adam wanted to check if it was Ron. He thought about getting his parents, contacting a park ranger, or even calling 911. *No way,* Adam then thought, knowing Ron could get up and be gone, this time perhaps forever. Adam made a small loop, going off to the right to see if the man really was Ron. He saw the front of the man's shirt even though the man was looking the other way, toward Old Faithful. The gray sweatshirt said WYOMING on the front just above a buffalo face, and the hiking boots, although they had a bit of mud on them, were the same ones Adam had seen the day they climbed Devils Tower.

The man turned and looked in Adam's direction.

It is Ron! Adam thought to himself. *And I can't let him out of my sight!*

Buying Time at Old Faithful

Ashley sat down in front of her parents.

"Where's your brother?" her mom asked. "Isn't he with you?"

"No, the visitor center got packed all of a sudden," Ashley said. "We agreed to meet back here."

"It got crowded out here in a hurry, too," her dad said. "It looks like there are ten times as many people as when we got here. I think everyone who was walking around looking at the other geysers is here now, waiting for Old Faithful to do her thing."

Less than fifty yards away from his parents was Adam, who froze when Ron looked directly at him. After Ron turned away with no recognition in his eyes and appeared to be calmly surveying the area once again, Adam decided to walk toward him. When Adam got within a few feet, Ron looked up at him.

"Can I sit here?" Adam asked.

Ron didn't answer but shrugged his shoulders.

"Listen," Adam said quietly to Ron, sitting down next to him. "I'm Adam Arlington, and I know you. You're Ron Rapp. You might know that, but you might not know me. You were in a plane accident a few days ago, a really bad one, and I think you've got some amnesia or something from the crash."

Ron looked at him guardedly, not saying a word.

"My family is friends with your father," Adam said. "No one wants to hurt you. You're not in any trouble. We just all want to make sure you are all right. You're a guide at Devils Tower, a monument on the other side of the state. You helped me and my family climb it earlier this week. We put our lives in your hands, and you took care of us, helping us through a tough climb. Now, we want to help you through a tough time."

Ron still didn't budge, but he continued to stare at Adam. He looked both wary and confused, but finally he spoke.

"You know me?" Ron asked in surprise.

"Yes," Adam said. "You're a really nice person, and we've been trying to find you for almost a week. We nearly caught up to you when you got on a train in Guernsey, near where your plane crashed. And then we almost caught up to you again in Cody when you bought your tent and sleeping bag. A convenience store clerk who saw you in Thermopolis said your ear was bleeding. We were so worried about you. You might not want to go with my family and me right now, but at least let me get you some food or something."

Adam was trying to buy time, hoping his family would come down to where he sat with Ron. It was obvious Ron wasn't going to go anywhere with him. Yet Adam didn't want to risk leaving Ron to find his sister and parents. He feared the encounter might have scared Ron off. Ron could get up and walk away if Adam left him.

"Why are people looking for me?" Ron asked nervously. "Did I do something wrong?"

"No, no, not at all," Adam reassured him. "You just survived a plane crash. I can tell you there's nothing left of the plane—I've seen the wreckage. Somehow, you came out of it alive. You're just probably in a state of shock right now.

"Your dad was in a car accident. He's going to be fine, but he couldn't come out here," Adam continued. "We've talked to him on the phone every day, and he's counting on us to find you because he loves you very much. He's very scared right now. We're worried about you, too."

"Is my mother worried?" Ron asked. "I told her I was coming here to be a park ranger."

Adam didn't know what to say. But he had always told the truth in the past, and now was not the time to experiment with anything else.

"Your mother died six years ago of cancer," Adam said. "She was a really wonderful person."

Ron looked down at the ground in dismay.

Just then Old Faithful went off. The water soared into the air, and Adam could feel the mist courtesy of a wind from the west. The geyser kept going off, the water shooting higher and higher, as people gasped and snapped pictures. As Old Faithful slowed down, Ron looked at Adam.

"Maybe if I talked to my father, I would understand all this better," Ron said slowly. "I'm not feeling very well."

"Everything will be all right," Adam said. "We'll take great care of you and help you see your dad. You'll be just fine."

Mr. and Mrs. Arlington were worried about Adam. The crowd would dissipate as soon as Old Faithful was done, but they didn't want to wait that long to find him. As the geyser wound down its show, they got up with Ashley, walking in the direction of the gift shop.

Ashley looked to her left and caught a glimpse of Adam.

"Look, he's right there," Ashley said. "And that's Ron with him!"

They approached the two, who were facing each other. They didn't want to jolt Ron, so they announced their presence when they were still several feet away.

"Hi, Ron, hi, Adam," Mr. Arlington said. "We were worried about *both* of you this time."

Adam smiled and reintroduced everyone to Ron.

"I'm Anne, Adam's mother," Mrs. Arlington said with a smile. "With what you've been through, you must be exhausted. You're probably hungry, too. We've got some water and fruit here if you think you'd like anything."

"That would be nice," Ron said. "I haven't eaten much the last few days."

Ashley pulled a banana and a bottle of water from her backpack.

"Is your ear bothering you?" Mrs. Arlington asked. "Someone who saw you earlier this week told us it was bleeding."

Ron didn't say anything, but nodded as he ate.

"It's possible you suffered a concussion," Mrs. Arlington said. "Do you remember anything about the crash?"

Ron shook his head no.

"We need to get you to a hospital," Mr. Arlington told him gently. "We need to call you an ambulance."

Ron started to pull away from him suddenly, with a frightened look on his face.

"It's all right," Adam said. "My family and I will go with you. We won't leave you alone there, I promise."

Ron calmed down a little.

"Okay," Ron said. "But only if you'll stay with me, Adam."

"I will—you can count on it," Adam replied.

Mr. Arlington took out his cell phone and called the park rangers, asking them specifically not to use their siren or lights because of Ron's fractured emotional state. They sat on a bench and Ashley went to the parking lot to brief the ranger and the emergency medical technicians, or EMTs, on Ron's condition and warn them that he might panic if he were spooked. Then Ashley brought them to Ron.

"My son and I will be riding with Ron to the hospital," Mrs. Arlington told them. "Will that be all right under the circumstances?"

"Yes, ma'am," the male EMT said.

"We need to put you on this stretcher," the female EMT said to Ron. "Your friends will be right next to you the whole way. But we need you to lie down so you can save your energy and warm up. We have to get a better look at you."

Ron looked at Adam and grabbed his arm.

"It's all right, Ron," Adam said, trying to ignore the pain of Ron's well-muscled grip on his arm. "They couldn't pull me away from you if they tried."

The strong man's grip relaxed a little, and so did Adam's expression.

Adam took Ron's hand as the EMTs helped him onto the stretcher. Mrs. Arlington walked on his other side as they wheeled Ron to the ambulance.

"We'll be right behind you and meet you at the hospital," Mr. Arlington said. His wife waved to acknowledge that she had heard. They headed to the hospital, and the doctors there ran a battery of tests on Ron.

He had a serious concussion, but his bleeding was from a ruptured eardrum.

"They'll probably keep him sedated," Mrs. Arlington said when she and Adam came out of the emergency room. Just then, Mr. Arlington and Ashley, who couldn't bypass traffic like the ambulance on the way to the hospital, walked into the waiting room. Mrs. Arlington briefed her husband and daughter concerning what had gone on, and then a doctor came out.

"Is one of you Adam?" the doctor asked. Adam stood, and the doctor said, "He's heavily sedated, but he's asking for you again. He knows we're going to fly him to the hospital in Casper. But he wants to talk to you first."

"Doctor," Mr. Arlington said. "I can get Ron's father on the phone if you could talk to him now."

"Great," the doctor said. "I'd like that very much."

Mr. Arlington called Mr. Rapp and updated him about Ron. Then the doctor took the phone and told Mr. Rapp that they were going to move Ron to the hospital in Casper in an hour or so via helicopter. Ron's father relayed that he was getting out of the hospital and would be in Wyoming on a charter by morning to be with his son. The Arlingtons were elated at all the good news.

Adam walked in the same door the doctor had just exited and saw that Ron had more color in his face already. He had an IV tube in his arm and a bandage on his head.

"You doing okay?" Adam asked.

"I've been better—I do know that much," Ron said groggily, managing a smile.

"They just got your dad on the phone, and he's going to be out here tomorrow," Adam said. "There's a bigger hospital in Casper, and they have a specialist there who will see you. They told me you're going to be just fine, but because of all the shock and trauma your body has been through, they'll have to keep you in the hospital for a few days."

"Actually, that sounds good to me," Ron said. "It feels really good to be warm and lie down."

Adam smiled.

"You know, I won't see you again until after you see your dad tomorrow," Adam said. "Since it's late, we're only going to drive to Cody tonight. We'll go back to our motor home in Casper tomorrow and should be there by the afternoon. But I'll come to see you at the hospital in Casper as soon as we get back, I promise you that."

"Thanks for helping me. I'll see you tomorrow, Adam," Ron said sleepily. "I think I'll be all right . . . " he tried to finish, but began to doze off under the sedation.

Adam came out so Ron could rest, and told his family what Ron had said and how much better he looked. "I don't think he'll be walking off and disappearing with the medicine he's on right now," Adam laughed. "I'd say he's safe for tonight!"

"Wow," Mr. Arlington said. "To survive that crash the way he did is amazing."

"You know, it really is," Mrs. Arlington said. "I'm sure they'll keep him in the hospital until his memory loss fades some more. But he certainly is lucky."

The Arlingtons were going to Cody to stay in a hotel that night, even though they had just bought a replacement sleeping bag that day.

"With all we've been through finding Ron," Ashley said, "if you guys were going to have us camp out tonight, I was going to offer to splurge for the hotel room myself."

Everyone laughed as they drove out of the hospital parking lot and headed to Cody.

The Pilot's Puzzle Pieces

The following morning the family went for a long walk around town and had a big breakfast at the hotel's restaurant before starting the drive back to their motor home in Casper. They called the hospital as soon as they arrived to see if they could visit Ron. While they were disheartened to be told no because the FAA had just interviewed Ron and sapped his energy, the Arlingtons were relieved to hear that Ron's father had arrived and was in his son's room keeping him company.

Later that night, the phone rang at the motor home. It was Tom Rapp, inviting the Arlingtons to the hospital the following day.

Ron was conscious when the Arlingtons went into his hospital room the next morning. It was hard to tell who looked worse—Ron or his father, who was leaning back in his wheelchair with his outstretched leg in a cast, resting on the floor instead of the wheelchair's metal footrest. Ron had a bandage on his head with a concentration of gauze behind the ear that had been bleeding. Despite the bandages, he was clean shaven and looked a lot better than the last time the Arlingtons had seen him.

The family shook hands with Ron again, and Mr. Arlington leaned down to hug Ron's father.

"I can't tell you how much everything your family has done means to Ron and me," Mr. Rapp said. "It is just incredible. You helped the investigators save Ron's life. If it weren't for you, Ashley and Adam, tracking him down through the contact you had with that convenience store cashier in Thermopolis and then the construction workers in Meeteetse, my son wouldn't be here today."

Mr. Arlington put his arm around Adam, and Mrs. Arlington patted Ashley on the back.

"We're just glad you're all right, Ron," Adam said. "Have you talked to anyone about the whole experience?"

"I met with Julie Mitchum and the FAA investigators yesterday for about four hours. I was just starting to talk to my father about it when you all got here," Ron said.

"Oh, we're sorry—we'll just be on our way then," Mrs. Arlington said.

"No, I didn't mean that," Ron said, smiling. "You all should actually stay here. You might be able to help me fill in a few holes here and there, because not all of it is coming back to me that clearly right now. But I will tell you what I told Julie Mitchum and her investigative team."

"Okay," Mrs. Arlington said. "But if you'd feel better if we left you alone with your father, let us know."

"All right," Ron said. "I started remembering bits and pieces of things the day I met the construction workers.

Just about the crash, really. Each day I started remembering more and more. But it was just yesterday when I started putting it all together. I think the puzzle pieces are all beginning to fall into place in my head.

"I talked to Julie Mitchum about the crash this morning. Man, it was awful—but it could have been worse, much worse. I lost the power to all the controls in the airplane—no power at all. My radio was completely out. I couldn't even hear any static. My first thought was Camp Guernsey, but I could see as soon as I passed over it that it was pandemonium down there because the reservists were showing up. There were planes and choppers parked everywhere. And, really, I didn't know if I could bring the plane down safely there. If I missed at all, I would have endangered several of those people. I knew I had a little fuel left and that if I crashed at that point, it might start a fire. So I managed to circle around and come back to the north, heading to a higher altitude because planes burn more fuel at higher altitudes than they do at lower altitudes."

"That explains why you hit the hill's south face," Adam said.

"Yes, it sure does," Ron said. "I climbed about 5,000 feet higher, and the plane was fighting me every step of the way—remember, I had almost no power at all, so these were manual maneuvers. I looked down and saw that I was over Guernsey State Park. I know the park pretty well because my friends and I have hiked there.

"I felt a sputter and then another. One more surge of fuel, and then the engine quit. I knew I couldn't do anything more with the plane at that point, whether I stayed up in the air with it or went down with it. I had a parachute, but I was nearly out of time at that point. I pulled it out of my backpack and put it on. Without even rezipping my backpack, I put that on my chest—backwards because I had the parachute on my back. Anyway, I had taken my wallet out when I was taking off to check a flight number on a card, so I forgot that. I got the plane as level as I could, and then I pushed open the door. Man, that door was so hard to open with everything else going on, and I had spent a lot of energy keeping the plane in the air long enough to find a safe place to put it down. I jumped out, and the next thing I remember is hitting my head—I think it was on the wing when I jumped. I didn't have my helmet on because there was no time for it—I barely managed getting on my chute as it was.

"So, I jumped out, hit my head, and that's it—lights out. Looking back, it could have been anywhere from a few minutes to a couple of hours before I came to. I landed way over near the rail yard in Guernsey. But I had no idea what had happened. It wasn't exactly a controlled landing for me or the plane. But at least we had made it to an area where we wouldn't come down on top of anyone else."

"You must've had no idea who or where you were," Mrs. Arlington interjected.

"Exactly," Ron said. "You don't know what a scary feeling that is. I didn't have my wallet, because it was still in the plane when it went down. I lost most of the clothes I had in my unzipped backpack on my way down, apparently. Thankfully, my chute opened all right. I'm guessing that I just let go of it when I conked my head. I must've gotten down to the ground pretty quickly, and the wind was strong, which explains how I drifted east all the way to the train yard. But, again, I was lucky. I didn't have any major injuries."

"Except a head wound that left you bleeding," Adam said.

"Oh, yeah, that, and I know now how serious that was," Ron said. "But I didn't have any broken bones or anything like that from my landing, so I was able to get away from the busy railroad tracks."

"But you didn't even know who you were," Ashley said. "It almost would've been better if you had broken a leg or something like that to immobilize you, so someone could've found you and gotten you medical help right away."

"You know, you're right," Ron said. "You don't know how badly I was freaking out at that time. I heard all those sirens and saw all kinds of police cars, and I had no idea who I was. So, I got really paranoid. Since I didn't know what I was doing there, I figured those police were all looking for me."

"Which," Adam said, "they were. Just not for the reasons you wondered about at that time."

"Bingo," Ron said. "So, I hid the parachute—that's why none of the searchers spotted it. And I hopped on the first train I saw, and then I took another. During one stretch along the highway, I saw a sign for Yellowstone National Park. I remembered that name because my parents took me there in the summer three or four times when I was little. I remembered all the trees and the big lake—even the geysers. But at that point, all I remembered was the place—I couldn't recall my parents or anything else at all. I just had memories of Yellowstone having a lot of wilderness areas where you could get really lost. In my confusion that's what I wanted to do, get really lost so no one could find me. I needed time to think and try to figure out what was happening to me or what I'd done to cause the authorities to be looking for me."

"But you couldn't even find yourself, and you would've probably died eventually," Ashley said. "How would anyone else have ever found you?"

"That's another good question, Ashley," Ron said. "But you have to remember that, at that point, I didn't want anyone to find me. I was fortunate because I had about $160 cash in my pocket for the trip to Cheyenne the night of my crash. Even though I didn't have my credit cards or anything, I had just enough to survive. I picked up a sleeping bag and a two-man tent in Cody. I got to Yellowstone by catching a ride with someone I met at the store when I was buying the tent. He and his friends were going there, and I said I was, too, but I didn't have a ride. He offered, and I accepted.

"We got there, and they went to a campground. I saw Yellowstone Lake, and the memories started coming back a little piece at a time. I hiked down along the shore and right where no one would see me I set up my tent and sleeping bag. I decided to get some food, and then I was going to stay in my tent indefinitely—at least that was my plan. I started walking west, and I could smell it—the sulphur."

"Just like at Thermopolis," Adam said. "The hot springs have that sulphur smell."

"Same thing," Ron said with a nod. "I headed out to the geyser basin, hitching a ride on the way, and that sulphur smell took me back to when I was a kid seeing Old Faithful for the first time. That's what I remembered. And, of course, you all found me a little while after I had gotten to Old Faithful."

"Incredible," Mr. Arlington said. "It's just amazing that you survived the crash and then survived that wild journey. You've had quite a week, young man."

"I'm not kidding myself," Ron said. "I know I might not be alive if it weren't for you all. The searchers and investigators did a wonderful job, but you often need help from family in cases like this. Since Mom is in heaven and Dad was taken out of action after his car accident, I had to have someone who was like family looking for me here, since I didn't know who 'me' was. You took on the role of my family, and I'm more grateful than words can describe."

"I agree," Mr. Rapp said, grabbing Mr. Arlington's right hand and Mrs. Arlington's left hand. "There's nothing I can say to express my gratitude. Ron is my only child, and since his mother has passed, we've had only each other. I'm so proud of him, and I can't imagine what life would be like without him. If it weren't for the four of you, I would be alone, and this wonderful young man wouldn't be here."

"We're glad to have played whatever role we did," Mr. Arlington said. "We know you'd do the same for one of our children."

"In a heartbeat," Ron's father said.

The phone rang in the room, and Mr. Rapp answered.

"Really?" Mr. Rapp said. "Well, that's great. At noon? Sure, we'll be there. Well, yes, I am proud of him. He did the right thing. Thank you, too. Good-bye."

"Who was that, Dad?" Ron asked.

"That was Julie Mitchum," his father said. "Because you risked your life to save the lives of those on the ground at Camp Guernsey, the FAA would like to present you with a certificate. The ceremony is downstairs tomorrow at noon."

"Congratulations," Ashley said, gently shaking Ron's hand. "We're proud of you."

"Will you come?" Ron asked.

Mr. Arlington looked at his wife, who nodded her head in agreement.

"We'll be honored to see you get your award," he said. "You deserve it."

After leaving the hospital so Ron and his dad could spend some more time together, the Arlingtons decided to head back across Casper to their campground.

"It's nice that we only have to go a couple of miles to see Ron now, instead of going clear across the state," Adam said with a smile.

After picking up a pizza, the Arlingtons ate outside the motor home under its awning. The evening wasn't nearly as chilly as it had been the previous few nights, so they stayed outside for a while.

"So, what did you two learn from this trip?" Mrs. Arlington asked, looking at Ashley and Adam.

"Oh, boy, here we go again. Might as well get it over with. Me first?" Ashley asked.

"Sure," Adam said.

"I learned that you can't judge things without knowing all the facts first," Ashley said. "Everyone—maybe even us to a degree—thought the worst when Ron first disappeared. There were allegations that maybe he was involved in some sort of criminal activity. The Wyoming law enforcement and FAA officials were very responsible. They didn't leak any of that to the media, and I really respect them for that, because they couldn't have kept those possibilities a secret back home in Washington, D.C.

"I mean, we had no answers for a long time to what had gone on. And when you speculate, you could ruin someone's career and reputation. Who could have guessed Ron would hit his head and forget who he was? If the suspicions had been printed, he would have been cast in a negative light. Yet, in truth, it turned out he was heroic, making sure his plane didn't go into the town and hit a residential neighborhood or school. I learned that you can't make a hypothesis—or at least you shouldn't—until you have enough evidence to let that guess stand on its own. We didn't have a hypothesis for days and days. And, as it turned out, no one's guess was right."

"That's great Ash," Mrs. Arlington said. "How about you, Adam?"

"You know, what Ron did was really amazing," Adam said after a long silence. "He risked his life to save people he didn't know, who could've been killed if he had bailed out when he needed to. Most of the people he saved don't know that yet, and maybe they will never know. But if Ron hadn't done it, there'd be a lot of wounds needing healing right now in Guernsey and Platte County. I could imagine a lot of people just jumping from an out-of-control plane and worrying about saving their own skins. I know the fear of dying isn't pleasant to think about, and I'd guess that most people don't think about it until they really have to. But Ron faced it and still put others' lives ahead of his own."

Mr. Arlington smiled. "You've both learned a lot; your mom and I are very proud of you and of Ron, too."

"I don't know what I would have done in Ron's place," Ashley said. "But maybe he didn't really know either, until it happened. Maybe if you just do your best every day, when a big decision comes along, you're ready for it."

Adam nodded, and they sat in silence a while longer and watched the stars appear.

Chapter 10

The Ranger's Reward

Mrs. Arlington woke first the next morning. The family ate a breakfast of yogurt and granola before taking off on a long bike ride. They then returned to the motor home and cleaned up for the ceremony at the hospital.

There was quite a gathering of people in the hospital lobby when the Arlingtons arrived. To make matters easier, everyone employed by a law enforcement or government agency was wearing a picture identification. Introductions were made, and the Arlingtons were able to once again come face to face with Julie Mitchum, whom they had not seen in person since they visited the crash site in Guernsey.

"It's good to see you again," Ashley said, shaking Julie Mitchum's hand.

"From what I've been hearing, you and Adam played a big role in this," she said to Ashley.

"Well, we did our best," Ashley said. Both she and Adam looked embarrassed at the praise.

"They're going to bring Ron and his father down here in just a second," Mitchum said. "If I don't get to spend any more time with you here today, stay in touch with me. You're special kids. You can e-mail me or call when you get home, just to let me know what you two are up to."

"I'd like that a lot," Adam said to her. "You have an interesting job, and I'd like to learn more about it."

"That's a deal," Mitchum said, smiling.

Ron and his father were wheeled into the room, side by side. Ron smiled and gave a thumbs-up sign to Ashley and Adam. Mr. Arlington went over and shook Mr. Rapp's hand. Julie Mitchum went to the podium and pulled out a piece of paper.

"May I have your attention please," she said to the gathering. "I'm Julie Mitchum, regional director for the Federal Aviation Administration. I think I've met most of you, and I'd like to thank everyone for being here. As you know, today we're going to present an award to Ron Rapp, who decided to put others' lives ahead of his own by making sure his troubled plane didn't crash into any populated areas."

She then presented the award to Ron. Mr. Rapp teared up listening to her tell everyone else in the room about his son's courage.

"In closing," Mitchum said, "I'd like to say this: Ron, you are an example to us all. You are proof that sacrifice can hurt, but with the reward comes healing."

Ron smiled broadly and stood without help getting out of his wheelchair.

"Thank you to everyone here," Ron said. "For all your efforts at the FAA, the park service, law enforcement agencies, and at the hospital—I thank you. To the Arlingtons, your actions and thoughts have a special place in my heart, and I look forward to calling you my 'family' for years and years to come. And to my father: You are the reason I made the decision that day with the plane. You taught me everything I know. You don't just decide on the spur of the moment up there in the air to do what I did. Doing the right thing comes from who you are—being a ranger has trained me to put others' safety before my own. But it also comes from the character your parents instilled in you growing up. Dad, you have been my best teacher, example, and friend since the day I was born, and you always will be. I accept this award on behalf of my father and my late mother."

Few dry eyes were left in the room when Ron finished speaking. The television cameras that had taped the award presentations were now being readied to record Ron's telling of his incredible journey from start to finish. The Arlingtons waved good-bye from across the room, trying to let Ron deal with the media. But he motioned the family over, and he hugged each of them. Mr. Rapp also shook hands with everyone and hugged Mr. Arlington, and they agreed to get in touch with each other back in Washington, D.C.

The Arlingtons pulled out of the hospital parking lot to enjoy the rest of their vacation, which they planned to spend in the Grand Tetons. Mr. Arlington turned on public radio, which was broadcasting Ron's press conference. After that concluded, a radio announcer came on the air with a news break.

"We've got a breaking story from near the Grand Tetons," the newsman said. "A small plane went down in the area early this morning."

Mr. Arlington looked toward the passenger seat at Mrs. Arlington, who turned around and looked at Ashley and Adam.

"But we're happy to report," the announcer said, "that no one was hurt and both the pilot and his passengers escaped without injuries."

The Arlingtons let out a collective sigh of relief. And for the next five miles no one stopped laughing.

Wyoming

Fun
Fact
Files

Wyoming

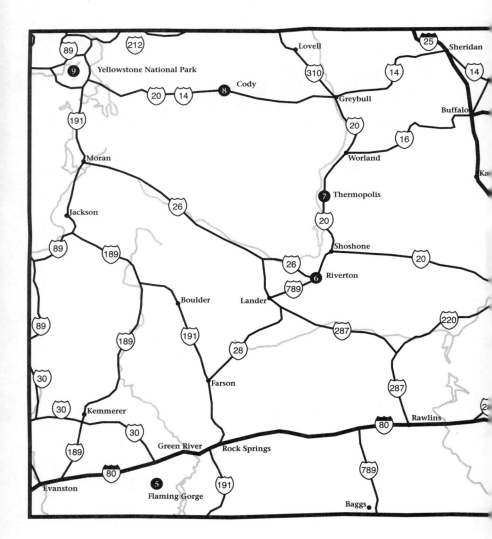

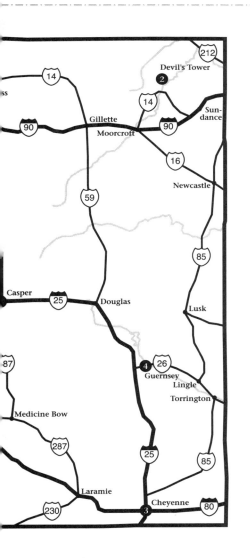

*The Arlingtons'
Route*

1. Casper
2. Devils Tower
3. Cheyenne
4. Guernsey
5. Flaming Gorge
6. Riverton
7. Thermopolis
8. Cody
9. Yellowstone
   National Park

Names and Symbols

Origin of Name:

Wyoming gets its name from two Delaware Indian words, which are translated "at the big flats," popularly thought to mean "large plains."

Nicknames:

Cowboy State, Equality State, Big Wyoming

Motto:

"Equal rights"

State Symbols:

flower—Indian paintbrush
tree—cottonwood
bird—meadowlark
mammal—bison
reptile—horned toad
gemstone—jade
insignia—bucking horse
song—"Wyoming"

Geography

Location:

Northern Great Plains/Rocky Mountains

Borders:

Montana (north and northwest)
South Dakota and Nebraska (east)
Colorado and Utah (south)
Idaho and Utah (west)

Area:

97,818 square miles (9th biggest state)

Highest Elevation:

Gannett Peak, in southwestern Wyoming's Wind River
Range (13,804 feet)

Lowest Elevation:

Belle Fourche River, Crook County (3,099 feet)

Nature

National Parks:

Grand Teton National Park
Yellowstone National Park (the first official National
Park—1872)

National Forests:

Bighorn National Forest
Black Hills National Forest
Bridger-Teton National Forest
Medicine Bow National Forest
Shoshone National Forest

Weather

Wyoming enjoys a generally cool and dry climate. However, it can get hot, with a recorded high temperature of 114 degrees. The lowest recorded temperature is 66 degrees below zero.

People and Cities

Population:

Wyoming is the least populated state, with a population of 481,000 (1998 census).

Capital:

Cheyenne

Ten Largest Cities (as of 1998)

Cheyenne (53,640)
Casper (48,283)
Laramie (25,035)
Gillette (19,463)
Rock Springs (19,408)

Sheridan (14,591)
Green River (13,059)
Evanston (11,475)
Riverton (10,126)
Cody (8,807)

Counties:

23 (plus Yellowstone National Park)

Major Industries

Agriculture:

Although Wyoming's climate is dry, agriculture is still an important part of the economy. Wyoming's shortgrass prairies provide cattle and sheep with plenty of grazing land. In 1995, only Texas and California produced more sheep and lambs, and Wyoming ranks second among the states in wool production. Other important crops are hay, sugar beets, wheat, oats, corn, potatoes, barley, and alfalfa.

Mining:

Mining is Wyoming's most important industry, its chief products being oil and natural gas. Wyoming has the world's largest sodium carbonate (natrona) deposits and has the nation's second largest uranium deposits. Other products include coal and clay. However, mining has taken a toll in some communities due to mining related pollution.

Tourism:

Tourists flock to Wyoming's many attractions, particularly Yellowstone National Park and Grand Teton National

Park. Besides scenic wonders, Wyoming has activities like rodeos, roundups, frontier celebrations, and dude ranches.

History

Native Americans:

The Crow first hunted the grasslands of Wyoming until they were pushed westward by the Sioux. The Sioux and other tribes, in turn, were troubled by the increasing numbers of settlers who entered the region after the Civil War, especially after the opening of the Bozeman Trail in 1864. Conflicts between the Sioux and settlers were common, but by the late 1870s, Native Americans had been largely subdued. The Arapaho were placed on the Wind River Reservation, while the Shoshone, their former enemies, moved their herds to grasslands throughout Wyoming.

Exploration and Settlement:

The middle to late eighteenth century may have seen the first Europeans in Wyoming. Most of these early settlers were French trappers and explorers. Parts of Wyoming were at one time claimed by Spain, France, and England, though none established much of a presence there. The first documented explorer was John Colter, who passed through Montana with the Lewis and Clark expedition then returned to explore the Yellowstone country in 1807. In 1812–1813, Robert Stuart pioneered the Oregon Trail through Wyoming. Fort Laramie was the first permanent trading post, built in 1834. It wasn't until 1867 that the first heavy influx of settlers came to Wyoming, lured by the discovery of gold at South Pass.

Territory:

Organized as Montana territory on July 25, 1868 (previously part of the territories of Dakota, Utah, and Idaho)

Statehood:

Entered the union on July 10, 1890 (44th state)

Check It Out

For more information about the places in this book, check out the following web sites and books.

Wyoming

Web site: http://www.state.wy.us/

Devils Tower

Web sites: http://www.newyoming.com/devilstower/
http://www.nps.gov/deto/

Rock Climbing

Book: Brimner, Larry Dane. Rock Climbing (First Book).
Danbury, Conn.: Franklin Watts, Inc., 1997.
Web site: http://www.extremesports.cjb.net/

Fort Laramie

Web site: http://www.nps.gov/fola/laramie.htm

Cody, Wyoming

Web site: http://www.codychamber.org/intro.htm

Buffalo Bill Cody

Book: Stevenson, Augusta, et al. Buffalo Bill: Frontier Daredevil (The Childhood of Famous Americans). New York: Aladdin Paperbacks, 1991.
Web sites: http://www.pbs.org/weta/thewest/wpages/wpgs400/w403_cod.htm
http://www.americanwest.com/pages/buffbill.htm

Buffalo

Book: Freedman, Russell. Buffalo Hunt. New York: Holiday House, 1988.
Web site: http://lsb.syr.edu/projects/cyberzoo/animals/americanbison.html

Yellowstone National Park

Web sites: http://www.forestry.umt.edu/yellowstone/
http://www.nps.gov/yell/home.htm
http://www.nationalgeographic.com/yellowstone/index.html

Geysers

Book: Gallant, Roy. Geysers:When Earth Roars (First Book). Topeka, Kan.: Econo-Clad Books, 1999.
Web sites: http://www.geyserstudy.org/geyser_main.htm
http://www2.wku.edu/www/geoweb/geyser/about2.html

Grand Teton National Park

Web site: http://www.nps.gov/grte/

Also Available . . .

Crime in a COLORADO Cave

0-8010-4453-7 $5.99

✖ In *Crime in a Colorado Cave,* Ashley and Adam, who are visiting Colorado's Cave of the Winds, join in the chase for thieves who have stolen a display of costly crystals. Will the pair be able to put the pieces together and recover the stolen crystals before the thieves escape?

Message in MONTANA

0-8010-4454-5 $5.99

✖ When the Arlingtons find a used game at a local store in *Message in Montana,* they also find themselves on the first step in an exciting new quest. The family follows the cryptic clues from city to city, learning about the Lewis and Clark expedition along the way. What they find will take readers by surprise.

SOUTH DAKOTA Treaty Search

0-8010-4451-0 $5.99

✖ In *South Dakota Treaty Search,* Ashley discovers a worn piece of paper in her new book, leading the Arlingtons to uncover the untold story behind the curious fragment. When they learn about an undisclosed government treaty, the family sets out to explore the Black Hills in search of the missing pieces of history.

Sports writer and newspaper editor **Bob Schaller** has won several awards for his journalistic excellence. Now a full-time writer, he is the author of The Olympic Dream and Spirit series, which covers athletes such as Mary Lou Retton, Dan O'Brien, Andre Agassi, and Dominique Moceanu. Schaller is also writing a biography of U.S. Olympic swimmer Amy Van Dyken. He lives in Colorado Springs, Colorado.